As his eyes traveled over the length of her, she felt as if she'd just been undressed.

"Well, if yc _____ e you should be _____ ur head, beca _____ dout in any circle,"

Tiana stared _____ ____ed. "Are you flirting with me?"

He spread his hands wide in innocence. "Just stating it like it is."

"In other words, you're flirting with me," she concluded.

Think again, she warned him silently. She didn't trust men, especially good-looking ones. "You can save your breath," she told him out loud. "I am much too rich for your blood."

He laughed softly. Brennan couldn't help being amused by her efforts to put him in his place.

"How do you know what I can afford? Maybe I've got a bulging...billfold," he concluded suggestively.

Her eyes narrowed. She was going to enjoy bringing the law down on this one, she thought.

Dear Reader,

In order to make a smoother transition for this newest member of the Cavanaugh family, this book picks up almost immediately where the last one ended. Saving former chief of police Andrew Cavanaugh's life caused undercover DEA agent Brennan Cavanaugh to blow his cover. That in turn got him assigned to desk duty by his unforgiving superiors. Brennan's restlessness causes him to find a new vocation in Aurora utilizing his former skills. He becomes an undercover vice squad detective trying to break up an interstate sex trafficking ring. His path crosses that of Tiana Drummond, a CSI detective from San Francisco who is trying to locate her missing younger sister, Janie. They join forces because two heads are better than one and they are running out of time.

Brennan's is the first of twenty-one stories, all of which belong to a long-lost branch of the family that Andrew was charged with finding for his father, Shamus. The latter wanted to be reunited with his missing younger brother, Murdoch. Murdoch, it turns out, is long gone, but his offspring and their children are alive and well. Hope you're as happy about this discovery as I am.

As always, I thank you for reading, and from the bottom of my heart, I wish you someone to love who loves you back.

Marie Ferrarella

CAVANAUGH UNDERCOVER

—

Marie Ferrarella

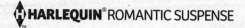

HARLEQUIN® ROMANTIC SUSPENSE

Recycling programs
for this product may
not exist in your area.

ISBN-13: 978-0-373-27869-5

CAVANAUGH UNDERCOVER

Printed in U.S.A.

MARIE FERRARELLA

This *USA TODAY* bestselling and RITA® Award-winning author has written more than two hundred books for Harlequin, some under the name Marie Nicole. Her romances are beloved by fans worldwide. Visit her website, www.marieferrarella.com.

To
My wonderful readers who wanted
To read about more Cavanaughs.
This newest branch
Belongs to you.
And to Alex Yu who
Told me his friend's name and
Made a character come to life.

Prologue

On his way home from the neighboring city of Shady Canyon, lost in his own thoughts, Andrew Cavanaugh smiled broadly to himself.

It had been a good, extremely productive and satisfying visit that had lasted a good deal longer than he'd first anticipated. Dusk had come and gone, and evening, with its long, engulfing shadows, had taken up residence along his route, allowing the hint of a fog to tag along, further intensifying the loneliness of this stretch of land.

It wasn't often that the former chief of Aurora's police department patted himself on the back for something, but this definitely was one of those rare times. Through his efforts of relentless investigation, he'd not only discovered the missing branch of his family that his father had charged him with finding, but made contact with them.

Contact? Hell, he made arrangements to have the entire bunch—and it *was* a rather large bunch—come out to his place a week from next Saturday so that they could get acquainted with a lot of family that they hadn't even realized existed.

Who would have thought that the missing branch of the family was only a city away? And that those members were all, just as they were here, entrenched in some form of law enforcement?

Andrew didn't normally believe in coincidences, but this, certainly, was a huge one.

It was a damn small world, Andrew thought, a deep chuckle echoing within the interior of his sedan.

He was really tired, but at the same time, he was very enthused and extremely pleased with the results of his relentless efforts. He'd called Rose before he left for home and shared the entire experience with her. She was as excited as he was about these new family members. She'd said that she couldn't wait to meet them. That was his Rose, he thought with a surge of affection.

No two ways about it, the woman was a saint to put up with an unending number of family members and still keep on smiling. There were women who would have the exact opposite reaction.

He'd ended the call by telling her that he was coming home tonight, but it might be late so she shouldn't wait up.

As if she'd listened to him, he thought with a soft

laugh. The light of his life listened to him when it suited her, did what she wanted the rest of the time. She always had.

It didn't matter. He was a hell of a lucky man and he knew it.

He—

Andrew's breath caught in his throat as he made out something up on the road just ahead.

The slight fog was beginning to settle in more intensely now, and visibility was definitely being challenged.

Damn, what *was* that, anyway?

Andrew felt for his shirt pocket. It was empty.

Where had he put his glasses? He should have worn them driving home tonight, but they made him feel old.

Hell, you are old, a voice in his head pointed out. As always, he ignored it. He wasn't twenty-nine anymore, but he was *still* in the prime of life. Old was destined to be fifteen years older than he was.

Always.

Andrew squinted. He was almost certain he saw someone staggering up ahead in the road. Not wanting to take any chances, he swerved at the last minute to keep from hitting it. As his car spun to the left, he struggled to regain control of it.

Andrew was so busy trying to steer into the spin, he didn't see the person in the middle of the road raising a gun until it was too late.

The single, resounding shot went into his windshield, shattering it.

The last thing Andrew Cavanaugh was aware of

was the windshield glass falling inside his vehicle like so many bits of fragmented snowflakes.

The pain in his chest consumed him, blotting out the entire world.

The bent, ragged, homeless man, who had appeared to have been so preoccupied with pawing through the overflowing trash cans that were lined up in the alley like so many drunken revelers, came to attention at the first sound of squealing tires. The vacant look on his face vanished as if it had never existed.

Eyes on the fishtailing white sedan in the middle of the deserted road, the undercover DEA agent heard the gunshot screaming through the night air and then saw the shooter hurrying toward the immobilized vehicle.

By then Brennan Cavanaugh stopped pretending that he was just a hapless spectator, interested only in his own survival, and was galvanized into action. He began sprinting toward the car and, more important, toward the victim he glimpsed inside it.

That was when the shooter obviously realized there was someone else in the vicinity besides the driver who had been presumably taken out by the well-aimed bullet.

Biting off what sounded like a livid curse, the shooter turned around and ran back into the shadows, seeking the cover of night. Undoubtedly focused on survival, the shooter didn't turn around one last time and so wasn't able to see the ragged man dragging the former chief of police from his car. Consequently, there was no second shot piercing the night air to finish the job.

Only the sound of running feet growing fainter.

Brennan checked for a pulse the moment he felt he and the victim were far enough away from the car in case it burst into flames.

It took him two tries, but he finally detected a pulse. An extremely faint one.

"Hang in there, mister," he told the unconscious man. "Don't die on me. Don't let me blow my cover and just possibly my whole career for no reason."

Feeling around in the deep pockets of his filthy khaki-colored hoodie with his left hand—his right was busy trying to stem the victim's flow of blood—Brennan pulled out his cell phone and called for an ambulance.

As he did so, he couldn't shake the strangest feeling that he was watching a chapter of his life slam shut.

And maybe, just maybe, another one creak open.

Chapter 1

"You've been nursing that beer for the last hour. Something bothering you, son?"

Brennan Cavanaugh was lost in thought as he leaned against the cool white stucco wall and watched people who constituted his newly discovered family enjoying themselves. It took him a moment to zero in on the man asking the question.

Brennan had an aptitude for names and faces—in his line of work, or former line of work, he corrected himself, he'd had to. He knew the man speaking to him to be Brian Cavanaugh, the Aurora police department's chief of detectives, younger brother of the man whose life he had saved, an act that had, as he'd silently predicted, terminated an active part of his own career, since he had to blow his cover in order to save Andrew Cavanaugh—his long lost uncle. He couldn't help thinking that truth could be a lot stranger than fiction.

"Not really," he replied.

It was the easiest answer to give. In his experience, when people asked how you were doing, or if something was wrong, they really didn't want to know and certainly not in detail.

But Brian obviously did not fall into that general category, because he pressed a little. "Fakely, then?" Brian asked with an understanding smile.

Brian knew all about people's reluctance to talk. He'd witnessed it initially from his early days on the force when he questioned victims and suspects. He was aware of it currently because of the office he'd held for a number of years.

Since becoming the chief of detectives, he had come across more than one person who was afraid to share his private feelings because he thought it might affected his work life adversely. Brian's gift was that he knew instinctively how to separate the two and how much weight to give to what he heard in both capacities: as the chief of detectives and as a relative/friend.

"All right, let's just say, for the sake of hypothetical argument, that there was something causing you some *minor* concern. What would that be?" he asked when Brennan made no response to his earlier joking comment.

Because he wasn't quite ready to talk about it, Brennan went with the most obvious answer. "I'll be the first to admit that I grew up in a crowd scene. Every holiday, birthday or miscellaneous celebration, there were always acres and acres of family—but this, well, this gives a whole new meaning to words like *overwhelmed.* I've heard of family trees, but this, this is damn near a family forest," Brennan quipped with a grin that took its time in forming.

Brian laughed. "You have that right," he readily agreed. "But at the risk of harping, that's not what's bothering you." He saw the suspicious way Brennan looked at him. "Don't look so surprised, boy. I didn't get to where I am on good looks alone." The statement was accompanied by another, this time deeper, laugh. "I'm a fair hand at reading people." And there was definitely something bothering this young man who had saved his older brother's life. Brian intended, eventually, to get to the bottom of it. "Now, if you don't want to talk, I understand. But if you do," Brian continued, "I am a good man to talk to. I listen."

Brennan shrugged as he stared down at the light that was being reflected in what was left of his beer. The overhead patio light shimmered seductively on the liquid surface, as if it were flirting with him.

"It's nothing, sir," he finally said. "I was just wondering what I was going to do with myself come Monday morning, that's all."

Brian appeared slightly puzzled. "I thought you were working undercover for the DEA. Something to do with drug smuggling."

Brian left the statement vague despite the fact that he knew exactly what the young man next to him had been up to when he rescued Andrew. The moment he'd done that, Brian had made it his business to find out everything he could about the tall, strapping DEA agent with the same last name.

Brennan nodded, avoiding his eyes. "I was."

"Was," Brian repeated as if he was trying to see if he'd heard the word correctly.

At the last moment, Brennan withheld a sigh. "Yes, sir."

Brian was about to tell the younger man not to call him sir, but he knew it would be a wasted effort, so he let it pass. "But you're not anymore." It was now an assumption.

Brennan frowned, though he thought it hid it. "No, sir."

"Case over?" Brennan asked. Obviously his digging hadn't turned up the whole story.

Brennan shook his head. "No, sir."

"I see," Brian replied quietly. And he did because all the pieces suddenly came together. "You blew your cover saving my brother."

Brennan didn't want any accolades. He'd done what needed doing. That it cost him wasn't the victim's fault. "I had no choice."

"Some people might argue that you did have a choice."

At bottom it was an argument that debated the responsibilities of a cameraman. Does he or she watch a scene unfold and film it as it happens no matter what that might be or interfere if what is being filmed depicts something immoral or illegal? Some felt it was their duty to record events as they happened; others felt duty-bound to come in on the side of right.

Brennan shrugged. "Doesn't matter what anybody argues. Way I see it, I didn't have a choice. He would have been dead if I just stood and watched."

Brian smiled and nodded. "Good answer—for all of us. So, does this mean you're currently out of a job?" he asked.

"Change of venue," Brennan corrected. "They put me on desk duty."

"Until we can trust you to keep your assignment foremost on your 'to-do' list and not play superhero, you stay behind a desk," Lieutenant Lisbon, his direct superior, had shouted at him. As fair skinned as they came, Lisbon had a habit of turning an almost bright red whenever he was angry and he had been very angry the day he'd thrown him off the case.

Brian looked at him knowingly. "Let me guess. You're not a desk duty kind of guy."

"Nope."

Brian didn't even pause before asking, "Have you given any thought to having a different sort of change of venue?"

Was the chief of Ds being philosophical, or—? "What do you mean, 'different'?"

Brian felt him out slowly, watching Brennan's eyes for his true response. "Let's just say going from the DEA to being a police detective on the Aurora Police Department?"

Brennan's electric blue eyes narrowed as he stopped taking in the people in the immediate vicinity and focused completely on the man he was talking to.

"Are you offering me a job, sir?" he asked a little uncertainly.

The politely worded question almost had him laughing out loud. "Boy, after what you did, you can write your own ticket to anything that's within this family's power to give, so yes, I am offering you a job. As a matter of fact, something recently came to my attention that you would undoubtedly be perfect for, given your undercover background."

Brennan could feel himself getting hopeful. He needed to nip that in the bud if this wasn't going to pan out. "You're not just pulling my leg, are you, sir?"

"I have been known to do a great many things in my time, singularly or on an ongoing basis. However, leg pulling does not number among them, so no, I am not pulling your leg."

Setting his own glass—now devoid of beer—aside on the closest flat surface, Brian turned his attention completely to the subject he was about to share with this new member of the family.

"Word has it that we've had more than our share of runaways lately. There have always been one or two in a year. However, the number went up dramatically recently. Ten in two months."

"You don't think they're runaways?" It was a rhetorical question.

"I do not," Brian confirmed. Runaways were bad enough. What he was about to say was infinitely worse. "Rumor has it that these missing girls are being 'recruited' one way or another for the sole purpose of becoming sex slaves, used to sate the appetites of men whose sick preferences tend toward underaged girls. Preferably untouched underaged girls. I'm putting together a task force to track down the people in charge of this sex-trafficking ring, and I could use a man like you on the inside to do what you normally do."

"And that is?" Brennan asked, curious as to how the chief perceived him.

"Get the bad guys to trust you," Brian said simply, humor curving the sides of his mouth.

This definitely sounded as if it had possibilities and it certainly beat the hell out of sitting behind a desk, aging.

"Who would I have to see about applying for the job?" Brennan asked.

"You're seeing him," Brian assured him, then Brian laughed softly to himself as he shook his head and marveled, "Who knew it would be such a small world and that someone from the very branch of the family that Andrew set out to track down wound up saving his life." Brian straightened, moving away from the wall. "I guess that's what they mean when people talk about 'karma.'"

"Maybe," Brennan allowed.

He certainly had no better or other plausible explanation for why he'd been where he was that fateful night. He hadn't even known that his late grandfather had had any family other than the four children he had fathered.

The life Brennan had chosen didn't allow him to make any unnecessary contact with anyone from his "other" life for months at a time. Since he wasn't married and his last semimeaningful relationship was far in the past, he was a perfect candidate for the job he'd had.

Emphasis, Brennan reminded himself, on the word *had*.

Brian grinned at him as the man straightened and indicated a keg several yards away. "Let's see about getting you that refill now," he prompted.

Brennan looked down at the glass he was holding and noticed that it was empty. Without realizing it, as he'd talked to Brian, he'd consumed the rest of the beer.

He flashed a grin now and said, "Sure, why not?"

Brian clapped an arm around his shoulders, directing him toward the keg. "Can't think of a single reason," he confirmed. "Let's go."

"A little overwhelming, isn't it?" the tall, broad-shouldered man who had joined Brennan nursing something amber in a chunky glass, asked, amused.

The dinner had been served and now everyone had broken up into smaller groups, some remaining in the house, some drifting outside. All in all, Andrew Cavanaugh's "get acquainted" party was teeming with Cavanaughs. Brennan was still trying to absorb everything that his chance action several weeks ago had brought about.

So many names, so many faces, he couldn't help thinking.

Brennan looked now at the man who was addressing him. They were around the same height and there was something vaguely familiar about him.

Or maybe it was that the amicable man looked a great deal like the lion's share of the men who were meandering about the house and grounds, talking, laughing or, in some instances, just listening.

"You could say that," Brennan agreed.

"Don't be shy about it. First time I attended one of these 'little' family gatherings, I thought I'd wandered into a central casting call for Hollywood's answer to what a family of cops was supposed to look like."

"The first time," Brennan repeated, having picked up the term. "Does that mean that you're *not* a Cavanaugh?"

"Well, yeah, actually, I am," the other man more than willingly admitted, then grinned as he remembered the confusion that had ensued over this discovery coming to light. "But at the time, I thought I was a Cavelli."

If this was some kind of a riddle, it left him standing in the dark. "I'm sorry, but I just don't follow."

Thomas laughed. "At the time, neither did I. I'm Thomas," he said abruptly, realizing that he *hadn't* introduced himself.

Shifting his glass to his other hand, he offered it in a handshake, which Brennan easily took. "Brennan," Brennan told him.

The expression on Thomas's face told him that he didn't need to make the introduction. His name had made the rounds. "My father's Sean Cavanaugh, the—"

"—head of the daytime crime scene investigative unit," Brennan completed. "I looked over the roster at the department before I came here." Even so, he couldn't untangle the confusion associated with what Thomas was telling him. "But if your father's a Cavanaugh, then I don't—"

Thomas decided to tell this story from the beginning. "There was a time when he didn't know he was a Cavanaugh. You notice the strong resemblance between my father, Sean, and the former chief of police, Andrew—the guy whose life you saved," he added.

Brennan nodded. "Yeah."

"Well, so did a lot of other people a few years ago. They thought that the chief was snubbing them and flat-out ignoring them. Since he was doing no such thing and wasn't even in these places they claimed to have seen him, he did a little detective work of his own to see if he could track down this man who supposedly had his face.

"That led to tracking down a few important details—like where he was born, when, all that good stuff. Turns out that the day my dad was born, so was another male baby. And if that wasn't enough of a coincidence, they were both named Sean. One was a Cavanaugh and the other was a Cavelli—Two *C*s," he emphasized.

"And let me guess, the nurse got them confused."

"Give the man a cigar. Story goes she'd just been told her soldier fiancé had been killed overseas by a roadside bomb. She was completely beside herself and just going through the motions to keep from collapsing in a heap. To add to our little drama, the infant the Cavanaughs brought home died before his first birthday."

"I guess that trumps a divorce and estranged brothers," Brennan quipped.

Thomas held up his hand, indicating that he not dismiss the matter so quickly. "Not when the reunion brings twenty-four more Cavanaughs to the table." He laughed.

Brennan looked around. He knew that all his siblings and cousins, not to mention his father, aunt and uncles, hadn't all been able to make this gathering. Despite that, it *still* looked like a crowd scene from some epic, biblical movie.

"Just how many Cavanaughs *are* there?" he asked, looking at Thomas.

"You asking about Cavanaughs strictly by birth, or are you including the ones by marriage, too?"

Brennan shrugged. "The latter, I guess." He'd heard that once you entered the inner circle, you were a Cavanaugh for life.

"Haven't a clue," Thomas admitted honestly, keeping a straight face. "But I'm betting we could have easily had enough people to storm the Bastille back in the day." The oldest of the Cavanaugh-Cavelli branch—not counting his father, Sean—Thomas grinned as he raised his glass in a toast to Brennan. "Welcome to the family."

Brennan laughed. "Thanks," he said, draining his own glass. Being part of what was perceived to be a dynasty felt rather good from where he stood.

Tiana Drummond didn't pray much anymore.

It was an activity she'd given up even before her

father, Officer Harvey Drummond, had died. There didn't seem to be much point in engaging in something that never yielded any positive results.

The official story given out about her father's untimely demise was that he'd died on the job, in the line of duty. That, strictly speaking, was true—as far as it went. But the whole truth of it was that her father had died *because* he'd been drunk while on duty and it had drastically robbed him of any edge he might have had. Drawing his weapon faster than a punk bank robber hadn't even been a remote possibility and consequently, Officer Harvey Drummond had died by that bank robber's hand.

At the funeral—a no-frills version mercifully paid for by the patrolmen's union—she and her younger sister, Janie, had heard glowing words about a man neither one of them recognized, much less knew. It was the way his fellow officers on the beat knew him.

The father that she and her sister remembered was a man who'd been both too bitter and too strict to do anything but give them the minimal basic shelter while trying to verbally and physically break their spirits every opportunity he got. For her part, rather than run away from home the way she'd been tempted to do more than once, Tiana had done what she could to protect her sister. She got between her father's punishing hand and Janie time and again. Some of the scars didn't heal.

Harvey Drummond blamed both of his daughters for the fact that his wife had left him, disappearing one day while they were at school and he was at work. Sylvia Drummond had left nothing in her wake but a note secured by a fish-shaped magnet to the refrigerator that said "I can't take it anymore."

The note had been written to him, but Harvey maintained that it was their behavior she couldn't take, hers and Janie's. He took his rage out on them every time he was drunk. Which was often.

Tiana and her sister endured hell on a regular nightly basis.

But once their father no longer walked among the living, life got better. Harder financially despite his pension, but better because she and Janie were finally allowed to pick up the pieces of their souls and do their best to reconstruct those pieces into some sort of workable whole again.

But the years they had had to endure with their father had left their mark, affecting them differently. Tiana, always self-sufficient, became more closed off. More distrustful of any man whose path crossed hers. Any relationships that looked as if they might have some sort of potential she quickly shut down before they ever flourished.

Janie, on the other hand, desperately craved attention, hungered for affection and was starved for approval—the three *A*s Tiana called them—and looked to any man hoping that he would provide her with them. Janie, Tiana had asserted more than once, was far too trusting, while Tiana only trusted men to stir up trouble and make situations worse. She knew that she wasn't being altogether fair in her estimation—but at least she was being safe.

Tiana would have been the first to admit that their late father was good for one thing—he had, without really meaning to, provided her with valuable connections. Connections on the police force. While Tiana had never wanted rules bent in her favor, she wanted to make sure that they weren't bent *against* her, either. All she had ever wanted was a fair shot at whatever she set her sights on. In this case, it was becoming part of the police department.

Eventually, while taking college courses on her computer at night, Tiana joined the San Francisco police force, managing to impress them with her physical stamina—another unintended "bonus" of surviving her father's brutal treatment.

Once she joined up, it wasn't long before she found her way to the crime scene investigative unit, a subject that had always fascinated her.

Every penny Tiana earned that didn't go to cover basic living expenses went toward Janie's education. Her only request was that Janie attend a college within the state so she could keep an eye on her. Janie was very disgruntled at what she perceived to be a restriction. "You're just like Dad," she'd railed.

The words cut her deeply, but Tiana had remained firm on this one condition. She had to since she felt that Janie, while not exactly outwardly rebellious toward her, was far too naive and prone to making bad judgment calls.

Like the boyfriend she'd gotten mixed up with, a supposed senior at the same college that seventeen-year-old Janie was attending—the University of San Francisco.

When she first met Wayne Scott, the light of Janie's life, Tiana had felt really bad vibes coming from this man. The occurrence took her by surprise because she generally didn't believe things like that were possible. There was just something about him; he was too verbally obliging, too ready to take her—Tiana—anywhere she wanted to go. There were a few times she could have sworn the college senior was actually coming on to her.

Tiana tried as gently as possible to encourage Janie to see other guys. But for her sister, the sun rose and set around Wayne's close-shaved head. Tiana instinctively sensed that the more she'd say against Wayne, the more Janie would defend him and dig in her heels, at the same time turning her back on the only family she had.

So Tiana had kept her peace and even refrained from saying anything when it became apparent that Janie was cutting classes to hang out with this loser.

But when one of Janie's friends called to ask if Janie had quit college altogether, all sorts of red lights and alarms had gone off in Tiana's head. When she asked around, it came to light that *no one* had seen Janie either in her classes or at the part-time job she'd gotten to help with her schooling expenses approximately two weeks ago. Sick with worry, Tiana only became more so upon learning that according to her room-mate, Janie hadn't been to her dorm room for those same two weeks.

And no one had seen her boyfriend, either.

Tiana immediately went into high gear to try to track down her sister's movements and current where-abouts. Accessing local cameras around the college and the places that her sister had frequented had ulti-mately yielded eyestrain and nothing else. For all in-tents and purposes, both Janie and her boyfriend had completely disappeared from the San Francisco area.

Tiana tried calling Janie on her cell phone both day and night to no avail. All her calls went straight to voice mail until finally, the metallic voice told her that the mailbox was full.

Growing increasingly desperate, Tiana tried to get coordinates on her sister by using the GPS feature of her cell phone. That had eventually gotten her sister's phone—abandoned in a Dumpster—but not her sister.

"C'mon, Janie," she had pleaded, glaring at the cell phone—an electronic fixture her sister would have never willingly thrown away. "Give me a clue, some-thing to work with. Anything. Where *are* you?"

And about that time the rumors regarding a white slave ring operating somewhere in the general vicin-ity, "recruiting" new faces or, more aptly, new bodies, began to circulate.

The moment she heard, a cold chill had gone down her spine. And she knew, *knew* this was the direction she had to go in.

Further investigation on her part pointed to the trail working its way down to the southern portion of the state. She had no jurisdiction outside San Francisco and she knew she'd be strictly on her own.

But since nothing in the world was more important to her than Janie, Tiana did what she had to do. She requested a leave of absence and took off that very day, following the only lead she had—a confidential informant who owed her a favor since it was her work in the lab that had eventually cleared the man of some pretty nasty charges. The informant told her that Wayne was mixed up with the traffickers.

When she was a kid, Tiana had prayed feverishly, seeking the help of a higher power. She had prayed that her mother would come back to take them away, out of her father's reach. She also prayed nightly that her father would change, suddenly regret the way he had treated them and do his best to make it up to her and her sister. Finally, all but devoid of hope, she still prayed that someone, *anyone,* would come to their rescue.

But their mother had never returned to take them with her, their father had continued to mistreat and abuse them—especially her—until the day he died and no one ever came to rescue them.

A week after their father was killed, Tiana turned eighteen and *she* was the one who rescued Janie. *She* was the one who stood up and did what had to be done, taking care of herself *and* her sister. And, since none of her prayers were ever answered, she concluded that there was no one listening. So she gave up praying.

She still didn't pray.

Faced with the huge challenge of tracking down her sister and bringing her home, Tiana saw no reason to go back to something that had only failed her time and time again. In this big, wide world, Tiana had discovered that the only person she could rely on with any sort of certainty was herself.

So be it.

She just had to gather her inner fortitude and her strength together. She intended to do whatever had to be done to find her sister. And if, along the way, she ran into Wayne, she felt confident that she could be forgiven for pummeling the worthless piece of garbage into the ground for having kidnapped Janie.

Tiana was convinced that was what had happened. He'd drugged Janie and kidnapped her. There was no other reason why Janie hadn't gotten in contact with her in two weeks. Always before, no matter what kind of an argument they'd had, she and Janie had never gone for more than a few days without getting in contact with each other. Neither one of them had ever held any sort of a long-term grudge, although this campus Romeo had definitely thrown a wrench into the works and caused an upsetting schism to form between them.

But this went beyond even that. Something was definitely wrong.

She could feel it way down deep in her bones.

"If anything bad has happened to Janie," Tiana

promised the missing Wayne between clenched teeth as she packed a few essential things, then threw the single suitcase into her car, "I am going to fillet you and make you wish you were never born."

Voicing the threat aloud didn't make her feel immeasurably better.

But it helped.

Chapter 2

Tiana held her breath as she walked up to the motel door. The faded, peeling gray door was in desperate need of a fresh coat of paint and number 13's 3 was hanging upside down, held only partially in place by a nail precariously inserted at the bottom.

The thought occurred to Tiana that the barely attached 3 might be an omen of some sort.

She dismissed the thought. Behind this door—hopefully—was the only lead she had to help her find her sister. By calling in every favor she'd had, she'd managed to get Wayne's credit card activity traced. The cocky dimwit had used his card to pay for his motel room, allowing her to trace him to this run-down twenty-unit motel.

With any luck, Janie was here, too. Tiana wasn't going to leave without the girl.

And if this lowlife had hurt Janie in any way, she would make sure he regretted it. Her sister was still a minor despite the fact that she was in her first year in college. Wayne was not. It was ultimately all the ammunition Tiana needed to have him put away.

Damn it, Janie, you're the smart one in this family. You're supposed to have more brains than this, running off with a loser. What were you thinking? Tiana silently demanded.

The next second, the direction of her thoughts did a one-eighty and anger turned to foreboding. *Please be all right, Janie. Please. I'll forgive this stupid lapse in judgment, just please be all right.*

Glancing around to see if anyone was watching—this unit faced the rear parking lot, which was at present devoid of any activity—she took out the small precision tools she needed to help her gain entry into the room. The last thing she intended to do was knock, alerting Wayne so that he'd wind up fleeing through the back window, dragging Janie in his wake.

But as Tiana inserted the thin metal tool into the keyhole, the door moved back.

It wasn't locked.

Tiana caught her lower lip between her teeth. She was either lucky—or something was very, very wrong.

It had been a while since she'd considered herself lucky.

Bracing herself, Tiana drew out her service weapon from its holster beneath her jacket. Her breath backing up in her lungs, she pushed the door open with her fingertips, moving it a painfully slow inch at a time.

The instant she saw Wayne spread out on the bed, she moved quickly, crossing from the entrance to the bed in less than a quarter of a heartbeat.

"Hands up, 'college boy'!" she ordered, aiming her weapon straight at him.

Wayne continued to lie exactly where he was, not flinching, not moving.

Nothing.

That was when the dirty bedspread lying beneath him finally registered with her brain. The bedspread was soaked with his blood. Tiana realized that he wasn't just staring into oblivion; his wide-open eyes no longer saw anything at all.

A wave of panic-fueled anger seized her.

"Oh, God, no, no, no. You can't be dead, you worthless piece of trash, do you hear me? You can't be dead!" she cried. "You have to tell me where Janie is!"

Wayne was her only connection, her only way of finding Janie. Biting off a curse, she pressed her fingers against his neck, searching for some sign of his pulse, faint or otherwise.

There was none.

Only blood that smeared against the plastic of the gloves she'd thought to put on before she'd entered—a habit from her day job where she'd learned to be very, very cautious about leaving crime scenes undisturbed.

This was surreal. It couldn't be happening. It couldn't!

Dazed, unable to process any thoughts, Tiana stared

at the dead man for a full moment, trying to pull herself together.

Now what do I do? her mind demanded. This waste of human skin was her *only* lead and he was dead.

Not only that, but he now represented a serious complication. What was she supposed to do with him?

She needed to call this in, but she couldn't very well stand around, waiting for them to arrive. She was going to have to make it an anonymous call to get them over here. Otherwise, there'd be too much to explain to them, and she didn't have time for that. All along, as she drove here, she'd been fighting an ever-increasing feeling of urgency. She just couldn't shake the feeling that she had to find Janie before it was too late.

There was this very real fear eating away at her that if she didn't find her sister soon, she never would. Victims caught up in the stranglehold of sex traffickers could vanish in an instant.

Yet she couldn't just leave this body here like this. It went against everything she was ever trained to do.

A compromise was in order. Since Wayne was already dead, Tiana decided that she'd call the police once she was well clear of here. From a pay phone—if she could locate one—so the call couldn't be traced back to her. She didn't have time for lengthy explanations or interrogations.

Returning her weapon to its holster beneath her jacket, she looked one last time at the person who had caused her so much grief. There was no pity, no sympathy for a life cut short. She felt nothing other than frustration. It occurred to her that she would have felt worse about any roadkill she encountered.

Crossing to the door, she threw it open, intending to run.

Only to find herself smack up against what would have been a solid brick wall had it not moved back even as it grabbed her by the shoulders.

Heart pounding as she tried to get herself together, Tiana simultaneously shook off the hold on her shoulders and pulled out her weapon for a second time in five minutes.

"Who the hell are you?" she demanded, anger usurping the fear she felt.

"Someone with a gun pointed at him," Brennan remarked, his hands partially raised out of respect for the weapon aimed at his chest.

He found himself looking even more intently at the petite redhead with wide blue eyes. But, despite her stature—was she even five two without those sexy-looking black stilts she was passing off as shoes?—she gave the impression of strength. Not the kind of outer strength that could easily lift heavy objects but the kind of inner strength that was able to move mountains.

Brennan had the impression that this redheaded powerhouse was a force to be reckoned with. And he found himself rather looking forward to that encounter.

Trained to make quick judgments, he swiftly took in the room, assessing what he saw. Sent only with the instruction to "tie up any loose ends" as a way of proving himself, he realized that he'd apparently walked into the middle of something unsavory.

"Mind pointing that somewhere else? You can point it at him," he suggested, nodding at the body on the bed, "since you seem to have already killed him."

The suggestion as well as his assumption took Tiana by surprise. "You think *I* shot him?" Pausing to review the scene, she knew how it appeared. She needed to do some quick explaining—if this man actually believed what he'd just said.

"Why not?" he asked rhetorically. "You're the one with the gun." As he spoke, he slowly lowered his hands, watching her intently as he did so for some sign that she'd shoot if he dropped them completely. "A woman can pull a trigger just as easily as a man— and then there're those neat gloves you're wearing—" he nodded at her hands "—so you don't leave any fingerprints. Looks like you've got all the bases covered." He cocked his head, as if daring her to prove his theory wrong.

"I'm cautious," Tiana countered, referring to the plastic gloves. "But he was already dead when I came in. I found him this way," she emphasized pointedly.

"And just how did you come to 'find' him in the first place?"

Tiana couldn't tell if the man she was talking to was a cop or part of the organization she suddenly realized she needed to track down. What she did know was that he was a lot bigger than she was and she had a feeling that he was pretty quick, as well. She might have a shot at outrunning him, but then what?

If he was part of the organization that dealt in sex trafficking, he might be her best shot at finding Janie. That meant making nice with him.

How nice?

Not that, she couldn't help thinking, being "nice" to this man would exactly be a miserable hardship, strictly speaking.

There was no doubt about the fact that the man was good-looking. Not the kind of good-looking that might be noticed peripherally in passing, but the kind of tall, dark and handsome good-looking that brought you to a jarring halt no matter what you were doing and had you staring, absolutely mesmerized by deep blue eyes that seemed to look into the most private corners of your soul.

Her mind scrambled for a plausible story. A kernel of an idea came to her. Utilizing it, she made up the rest of it as she went along.

"I have a phobia about catching something I shouldn't. These are just a precaution." She held up one hand as an illustration of her point. "I also like staying under the police's radar."

"Why's that?"

Her eyes on his, she carefully holstered her gun. It was a gesture of good faith—one she hoped she wouldn't regret.

"You a cop?" she asked.

Brennan laughed.

"Do I look like a cop?" he challenged, amusement highlighting a rather rugged face.

Tiana studied the stranger for a moment. He was

tall, dark-haired and broad-shouldered, not to mention rather impressively dressed in a gray suit that undoubtedly set him back a bit. They were making bad guys better looking these days.

"You've got the jaw for it," she quipped.

"But not the taste," he pointed out. "Mine's expensive," he explained. "A cop's salary wouldn't begin to pay for one of my suits." The corners of his mouth curved. "Okay, I showed you mine. You show me yours."

She realized he was alluding to being part of the organization. Here went nothing. "I'm new in town and looking for fresh talent."

"Him?" Brennan asked, a skeptical frown taking over his face.

Tiana laughed harshly. "Hardly. I came to talk to him because I'd heard that he was tied in to recruiting young girls."

The handsome stranger with the good bone structure raised an eyebrow. "You like girls?"

He was baiting her on purpose, she thought. Tiana kept her cool. "My clients do."

The raised eyebrow went up farther. "You're a madam."

She could hear the skepticism in his voice. This was her first hurdle and she needed to make a believer out of this man. If she didn't, she had a feeling that her foray into this dark world to extract Janie was doomed to failure right from the start.

"Yes, I am," she informed him haughtily. "Something wrong with that?"

"Hey, not mine to judge." He raised his hands as if to push the entire concept away. "But you are kind of dressed understated for a madam, aren't you?" he pointed out.

What was someone with her obvious good looks doing in a field like this? She looked too classy to be what she claimed to be. He could see her in a professional capacity—a *legitimate* professional capacity, not someone who dealt in flesh peddling.

But it took all kinds, he thought.

"I don't like to stand out when I'm out among civilians," Tiana told him.

He let his eyes travel over the length of her and could see her trying not to look away.

"Well, if you don't want to stand out, maybe you should be wearing a bag or a sack over your head, because your looks make you a standout in any circle," Brennan told her.

Tiana stared at him, stunned. "Are you flirting with me?" she asked incredulously.

He spread his hands wide in innocence. "Just stating it like it is."

"In other words, you're flirting with me," she concluded. She noted the lopsided smile gracing his lips. Undoubtedly the undoing of a lot of women and it made him feel he could just reach out and have anyone he wanted.

Think again, she warned him silently. She didn't trust men, especially good-looking ones. Her father had once been exceptionally good-looking, not to mention a charmer.

"You can save your breath," she told him out loud. "I am much too rich for your blood."

He laughed softly. "How do you know what I can afford? Maybe I've got a bulging…billfold," he concluded suggestively.

Her eyes narrowed. "It doesn't matter what you've got in your billfold. You can't afford me," she told him confidently.

He knew this was all about how successful he was at role-playing and posing. He needed to keep his mind on the game. That was what the chief was counting on, and he didn't want to disappoint the man the first time out.

All that taken into consideration, he admitted to himself that the woman in front of him made him itch. Itch a lot.

In a place he couldn't afford to scratch.

It was way too risky to do anything but banter with this low-key madam.

"You're piquing my interest," he finally told her.

"Well, you're boring mine."

"Sorry to hear that," he acknowledged. "I'll try harder next time."

"What makes you think there's going to be a next time?" she asked, sneering.

"Oh, lady, there's going to be a next time," he promised her. *One way or another,* he added silently, intrigued despite the situation. "Count on it."

Tiana narrowed her eyes. "You're part of the organization?"

He smiled, enjoying this game, even if the circumstances didn't quite call for it. Keeping her in suspense. "I might be."

"You either are or you're not," she said impatiently, her nerves just about at the end of their frayed life expectancy.

"What's it worth to you if I am?" he asked her, his eyes drifting over the length of her again.

She pushed ahead. "I'll pay top dollar for every girl I take off your hands—but they have to be in prime condition. No bruises, no scars, no signs of abuse. And teeth," she added. "They have to have teeth," she underscored. Tiana was doing her best to describe Janie the way she looked the last time she'd seen her. Hopefully, nothing of consequence had changed.

"Picky," he said.

"Thorough," she countered.

"That, too," he agreed. "Also very cool."

Her suspicions were immediately raised. "What do you mean?"

"I don't think I know many women—or many men for that matter—who could remain so calm around a recently murdered victim." He was studying her. "But you act as if this is an everyday occurrence in your world."

Tiana supposed that she did come off somewhat insensitive—not that she cared what this man ultimately thought of her unless it helped her find Janie—but she was far more concerned about the living. About her sister and other girls who undoubtedly had been stolen from their homes, from their parents who had to be as worried sick about them as she was about Janie.

As for her disregard of the lifeless body on the bed, well, to her way of thinking, Wayne had just gotten what he had coming to him. He'd stolen her sister, quite possibly stolen Janie's innocence, as well, and maybe even more than that. She had absolutely no tears to shed for the likes of someone like Wayne.

"I'm not interested in the dead," she told the tall stranger with the intense eyes. "My only interest is in the living. Now, can you help me or at least give me the name of someone who can? Because if you can't, then get the hell out of my way."

"All business, huh?"

She had the feeling he was baiting her, seeing how she reacted in a given situation. Why, she didn't know. Maybe it was some sort of a test. All she knew was that she wanted to wipe that smirk off his face. Badly.

"I left my warm, fuzzy center in my other outfit," she told him coldly.

"The one with the whip?" he asked with a straight face. Only his eyes showed any trace of humor.

"You've seen it," she deadpanned.

"Only in my dreams—" He hesitated for a moment. "So, what do I call you, anyway?"

If he was asking that, then maybe she'd passed whatever stupid test he was giving her. She never hesitated. "Aphrodite."

"The goddess of love," he acknowledged.

"You know your Greek mythology." She hadn't expected any of the people on the lower rungs of this organization to be educated. Maybe this man *wasn't* low man on the totem pole. Maybe he went up higher than that.

"I know a lot of things," he replied.

"Such as where the merchandise is being kept?" she asked, trying to sound vaguely bored as well as impatient. She fervently hoped her pounding heart wasn't going to give her away.

"Such as that, yes," Brennan said. Truth be told, he had just managed to breach the outer ring of the organization in this past week. He'd come to the traffickers, thanks to an informant who had since disappeared, only a few days ago, posing as a wealthy representative of a club that catered to depraved men who craved being serviced by females who were definitely below the legal voting age.

Because nothing was accepted at face value, his background—the background that had been created for him by Brenda Cavanaugh, the chief of Ds' daughter-in-law who ran the tech support division—was being checked out by unknown people even as he stood here, talking to this madam-in-search-of-an-extended-stable. He only hoped that Brenda was as good as everyone said she was. His life could very well depend on it.

"Then take me there," she challenged, moving in close to him.

"Whoa, hold your horses, honey," he warned. "Nobody sets foot in 'the candy store' without being checked out first."

"Like him?" she asked contemptuously, nodding her head at the dead college senior on the bed.

"I think it's pretty clear that he didn't make the grade," Brennan told her matter-of-factly.

"Was that why he was eliminated?" she asked, wondering why Wayne had been killed now rather than later. Knowing might help her find Janie. Every piece of information might very well be crucial—or not. It was like trying to navigate a moving van in a dense fog. She had no idea if she was going in the right direction, or completely off the road. She couldn't remember a time when she had been more frustrated.

"Part of the reason," Brennan allowed vaguely.

"Hold it," Tiana ordered as something dawned on her.

"If you knew he was already dead, why did you accuse me of killing him?" she demanded.

For a second he seemed flustered before quickly gaining his composure. "Simple," he said after a beat. "I wanted to see how fast you thought on your feet."

Incensed, because for a moment he'd had her thinking she was going to have to kill him in order to survive, Tiana gave in to her temper. She swung and made contact with his cheek—hard. The target of her wrath rubbed his cheek but refrained from saying anything or retaliating.

However, when the so-called madam began to swing again, he caught her wrist and held on to it just tightly enough to get his point across.

"The first one's free, on the house, so to speak," he told her. There was the hint of a smile on his lips, but his eyes were deadly serious. "Anything after that has consequences," he warned. His eyes narrowed as he looked into hers. "Understood?"

"Understood," she ground out grudgingly between clenched teeth. *Okay,* she thought. *Now I know how far I can push you.*

She dropped her hand to her side when he released it.

Chapter 3

It did surprise Tiana that the good-looking stranger was making no effort to leave the room. Most people wouldn't have wanted to share space with a corpse, yet he didn't look the least flustered. Since he appeared to be her only possible link to Janie, she couldn't leave until he did. She needed to have him take her to whoever he was associated with—and hope that whoever *that* was had a link to her sister.

"So now what happens?" she asked him.

"That all depends," he answered. He was still trying to figure her out. He'd already decided that the woman was a spitfire, but what else was she? Was she telling the truth about why she'd come to see the dead man, or was there something else going on? And just how was that going to affect the ultimate outcome of his assignment?

Like everything else he'd dealt with in the secret lives he'd had to undertake, Brennan decided to play it by ear.

"On what?" she asked.

"On who you're asking about. If you're referring to our friend here—" he nodded toward the dead man "—he stays right where he is. The motel maid will undoubtedly find him sooner or later and then he becomes the motel manager's problem."

"You're leaving him here?"

"Why not? He can't be traced back to anyone of consequence and since he can't hold up his end of the conversation, I don't see any point in taking him with me. Dead bodies are really a pain to get rid of," he told her.

The first second when no one else was around, he intended to call in and tell the chief of Ds about this latest casualty of the sex trafficking ring they were looking to take down. From everything he'd managed to put together, the man on the bed was nothing more than a would-be gofer for the organization. Someone who'd traded on his looks to get girls to follow him into the trap that was set for them. More than likely, he'd probably gotten an inflated sense of self and had asked for a bigger share of the profits. The answer to his demands was undoubtedly why his person was now sporting a bullet hole.

"If you're asking about me, I go back to where I

came from. As for you," he began as he looked down at her—and then paused.

The woman sounded a little impatient. "Yes?"

"Are you really on the level about looking for fresh talent?" he asked. His first instinct had been to cut her loose. His second was to keep her close. Maybe he could incorporate a little soul-saving into this assignment he was on.

She raised her chin again, appearing ready to go at it with him. "Why wouldn't I be?"

He laughed shortly. "You really want me to go into that?"

"That depends on how wild your imagination is."

His eyes met hers. If she really *was* a madam, he wondered what she'd been like, working her way up within the ranks. He knew better than to get involved, but it cost nothing to let his imagination go for a moment or two.

His mouth curved as his eyes swept over the length of her. "Pretty wild."

"Then no," she answered almost primly. "But I am on the level," she informed him. "Girls wear out fast in this line of work. And if they don't, they have an unfortunate habit of outgrowing it. My clients like them young and dewy fresh. The bloom only stays so long on the rose before it fades away."

Brennan nodded. "Your clients are fickle," he concluded.

"My clients are discerning," Tiana corrected him pointedly.

"Potato-po-tah-to," Brennan replied, waffling his hand

in front of her as if to say that he saw right through her protest.

He couldn't help wondering again what someone like her was doing mixed up in something like this. She looked too clean, too refined for the kind of low-life this sort of a trade usually attracted. They might have more money and have positions of importance in the everyday world, but her clients were still scum, just well-kept scum.

With no effort at all he could see this woman who'd given him such a phony name being a teacher or a shop owner, not someone who dealt in the misery of young women as she peddled their flesh to the highest bidder.

He wasn't here to get personally involved, Brennan reminded himself. Or to save a so-called fallen woman. The only people he was supposed to be concerning himself with were the young women who had been kidnapped or pressed into this life by being lied to. He was here to save them, not to get mixed up with a woman with electric blue eyes and hair that made him think of an out-of-control forest fire.

"I wouldn't look down my nose at anyone if I were you," she informed him. "It's not exactly as if you're without reproach here."

Brennan spread his hands in an exaggerated show of innocence. The smile on his face was positively wicked. "Never said I was."

"You haven't really said very much of anything, have you?" she accused.

Brennan didn't bother denying it. "Better that way. I make it a rule never to hand over the nails to my coffin to anyone. Never know when someone could use it against me," he told her.

"Well, not that I don't enjoy debating philosophy with you, mister…" She paused for a moment before asking, "What did you say your name was?"

Boy, was he enjoying this. "I didn't."

"Well, say it now," she ordered.

"Wayne," he said, drawling out the surname. "Bruce Wayne."

He had to be kidding. "Bruce Wayne," she repeated. "As in Batman?"

He heard the disbelief in her voice. He'd meant it as joke, but decided to stick to the name. For one thing, it was easier to remember. "My father had a sense of humor."

Her eyes took measure of him, from his head right down to the tips of his shoes. Okay, let him have his little joke. Maybe if she went along with it, Tiana thought, she could get closer to him. She needed some sort of a way in, and now that Wayne was permanently out of the running, this man was going to have to be it.

"Obviously," she agreed.

Not that she believed it for a minute. But it didn't matter what his name was. He could call himself Peter Rabbit for all she cared. As long as he provided her with a way to get to her sister, she'd call him any name he wanted.

"Not that I'm not enjoying this meaningless exchange," she went on to say, trying to light a fire under him and finally get out of this motel room, "but I'm kind of in a hurry."

"Don't be."

Was he putting her on some kind of notice? Or was there some other hidden meaning behind his words? She had no patience with riddles and puzzles, not when the stakes were so high.

"What's that supposed to mean?" she asked.

"It means that the man you're going to be dealing with holds people in a hurry suspect. You need to be laid-back."

That didn't make any sense to her. "Why?"

Roland, the man he'd dealt with, the one who had sent him out on what turned out to be a fool's errand, was nothing if not paranoid. "He might just think you're trying to set him up and are looking to put some distance between you before the trap goes off."

This Wayneman was getting too close to the truth. A lucky guess on his part? Or was she somehow transparent in her concern? Back in San Francisco she was a lab rat. She was damn good at her job but still a lab rat. Fieldwork wasn't exactly her specialty. She was winging this as she went along.

"I'm not trying to set anyone up," Tiana protested. "I just want to see if he has the kind of girls my clients prefer."

He raised his shoulders in a dismissive, disinterested shrug. "Just your word against his suspicions. You're better off acting like you have all the time in the world," he advised. "It sets off fewer alarms that way."

"But I don't have all the time in the world," she protested, getting further into her role. If Janie *was* being held captive by this sex trafficking ring, then she had no idea how much time she actually had before her sister was shipped off for parts unknown. The second Janie left the area, the chances of finding her fell abysmally. "I've got clients who'll take their business somewhere else if I don't bring them the kind of selection they're looking for."

"Somebody breathing's not enough, huh?" he asked her with a grin that she found hugely unsettling. It wasn't that it was creepy. What worried her was that it wasn't. Moreover, it got to her—which was totally unacceptable.

"Not even close," she told him. "They have very definite requirements." When he didn't say anything in response for a couple of minutes, just looked her over, she found it difficult not to shift uncomfortably. "What are you doing?" she asked.

"Making a judgment call."

He was judging *her?* Tiana squared her shoulders combatively. "And?" she challenged.

His expression was easygoing—quite the opposite of what she felt. "You pass."

"Good to know," she said in a bored voice. "Now will you take me to talk to someone in authority?" It was more of a demand than a request.

The amused, cocky grin widened. "What makes you think I'm not someone in authority?"

"Let's call it a hunch," she told him.

He inclined his head. She'd played that hand well. Whatever she was up to—and he was fairly certain she *was* up to something, something she was keeping to herself right now—she had guts. "Not bad. All right, I'll take you with me and introduce you to Roland."

"The man in charge?" she asked.

Brennan laughed shortly. There was very little humor in the sound. "He thinks he is."

Her eyes never left Wayne's face. She was looking for a chink in his armor, a tell she could use in her favor. There was nothing. "Is he right?" she asked.

Isaac Roland was far from in charge, although no one who worked directly for him would ever have had the nerve to tell him that to his face. The man in charge had yet to be identified, a fact that kept Brennan playing this charade. They needed a name in order to shut everything down and make their arrests.

"He's two rungs up the ladder," Brennan told her.

"What about you?" she asked. How did the man who called himself Wayne actually figure into all this? Was he the cleanup man, the guard at the door of an exclusive club who decided who gained access and who was turned away?

Or—?

"I'm the guy leaning against the ladder," he told her. The grin on his face made it impossible for her to gauge if he was telling her the truth or pulling her leg. And just what did he mean by that line, anyway? Was he saying that he wasn't part of the operation but just an interested spectator?

Or was he deliberately belittling his role in all this to gain her confidence and get her to talk to him? If so, to what end?

It was too much of a puzzle for her to solve now.

As long as he didn't pose any sort of an immediate threat—and she remained on her guard—she didn't care what he was in the scheme of things. Or who he *thought* he was.

On the surface, she seemed to be winning his trust—as far as it went—and right now that was good enough for her.

"If you're going back to him, I'll follow you in my car," she told him, about to leave the room. The dead man was making her feel claustrophobic.

Brennan caught her by the arm and she looked at him quizzically. She also spared a look at his fingers that were wrapped around her upper arm, her indication clear. The words *Let go* practically vibrated between them.

But he ignored the silent message and continued holding her forearm for a moment longer. "I think Roland would prefer it if we both used my car. He's very big on green energy and cutting down on pollution," he told her, his expression unreadable.

This "Roland" was also big on cutting back on avenues of escape, Tiana couldn't help thinking. But there was absolutely no way she could allude to that without raising all sorts of suspicions on the part of this man.

First she had to find Janie, *then* she could plan their escape, she told herself. The idea that, since Wayne was dead, Janie also might be dead, fleetingly visited her thoughts, but Tiana refused to allow it to take root. Janie was alive and she was here. Tiana refused to allow her mind to entertain any other possibility. To believe that her sister might be dead would render her completely inert. She'd be no good to Janie *or* herself that way.

Still, she knew she couldn't just docilely allow herself to be led away like some overgrown, directionally challenged lemming.

"What about my car?" she asked. "I can't just leave it here."

"Sure you can," he said. "I'll bring you back for it after you meet Roland and state the nature of your business to him."

Tiana knew she had no choice. If she protested, he'd just leave her here. Possibly in the same condition as Wayne was in. For that matter, she still wasn't a hundred percent convinced that this so-called Bruce Wayne wasn't the one who'd killed Wayne in the first place. The latter had always struck her as being almost too stupid to live, but discovering she was right was of no great consolation to her. He could have at least remained alive long enough to tell her where Janie was.

She struggled to contain her impatience and concern. "All right, have it your way, 'Bruce,'" she said.

Brennan flashed a quick smile in her direction. "I usually do." He said it without bragging or bravado. It was just a stated fact. "My car's right outside," he told her, finally leading the way out of the room. He paused to look around, as if to make certain that the area was still deserted. It was.

The sunlight seemed extra bright as she walked out of the dingy, dimly illuminated motel room, and she squinted for a moment, trying to acclimate her eyes to the pronounced change. In doing so, she didn't see the rock right in front of her. Stubbing the toe of her shoe on it, she tripped.

Instinct had Brennan reacting to the faint, telltale noises. He turned around just in time to catch her and keep the supple handful from making direct contact with the ground.

It all happened very fast, less than two beats of an old-fashioned clock, but even so, he was exceptionally aware of the softness of her body as it made contact with his.

As was she. He could tell by the very startled look in her eyes—which had flown wide-open.

"You make more headway if you keep your eyes open," he told her, amused.

"So they tell me," Tiana snapped, brushing herself off.

Since he'd caught her before she'd actually had a chance to hit the ground, he could only guess that she was attempting to symbolically brush away any trace of contact with him.

Was the lady protesting too much? he wondered. Or did she find him as compelling and intriguing as he found her?

"Car's right here," he pointed out.

Raising his hand, he pressed the security release on his car key. The silver BMW that had been recruited especially for this part he was undertaking softly whispered that its doors were now unlocked.

He waited until she opened the passenger-side door and got in before he followed suit himself on the driver's side.

She slid onto a seat that would have made butter seem unusually hard and brittle. Without thinking, she feathered her fingertips along the side of the seat appreciatively. "Business is good for you, too, I see."

The implication wasn't wasted on him. She was telling him that she was doing well in her chosen field.

"Can't complain," he said. He started the car with another press of a button.

"A person can *always* complain," she countered.

"Yeah," he agreed. "But nobody likes to hear complaints. Makes them unreceptive to the person. Me, I always believed in counting my blessings."

She looked at him in disbelief. Was this man for real? She couldn't decide one way or another. Her immediate gut feeling would have been to say no, but there was something about his tone of voice that told her she was being made privy to the truth, strange as it might sound.

"An optimistic pimp," she marveled as they left the parking lot behind them. "I don't think I've ever encountered one before."

"Then you need to broaden your social circles," he quipped.

Tiana pretended to think it over before she inclined her head. "Maybe," she allowed.

"And for the record," he told her matter-of-factly, "I'm not a pimp."

"A procurer?" she suggested. When he made no answer, she said, "Okay, what would you call yourself if you were filling out a résumé?" she asked loftily. "A matchmaker?" She laughed.

"A businessman," he corrected in all seriousness. "A pimp is someone who deals with the dregs of society, pushing them into the arms of their destruction for a hefty cut of their earnings."

She'd never heard it described *that* way. "You really *are* into philosophy, aren't you?" she marveled. "Either that, or you've learned just the right way to appease your conscience."

"Conscience has nothing to do with it," he assured her. Then, out of the blue, he asked her, "How about you?" When she looked at him quizzically, he elaborated on his question. "How did you get into this line of…work?" he finally said when the right word seemed to be eluding him.

"Quite by accident, actually," she answered.

"Explain," he urged.

"It's a long story for another day," she told him. *When I can come up with the story.* Out loud, she said, "When I know you better."

"We can take care of that little detail any time you say so," he assured her, his meaning made crystal clear by the smile on his face.

"I'll keep that in mind," she answered. *And I'll keep you at a distance. It'll be much safer that way,* she added silently, although she had a feeling that "safe," much less "safer," was not going to be something she would feel until she and Janie were as far away from here as possible.

And as far away from this man as possible, she added as an afterthought.

Chapter 4

The Aries Hotel with its understated opulence and its refined ambience was the complete opposite of the dingy motel where she'd tracked down Wayne. Tiana was confident that the average price of one room in the hotel was more than the combined sum gathered from all the rooms at the motel.

"What are we doing here?" Tiana asked, addressing the question to the back of "Bruce Wayne's" head as she followed him through the hotel's revolving door.

"You said you wanted to meet the man I've been dealing with," Brennan reminded her as he waited for her to join him.

"He's staying here?" she asked, scanning the immediate vicinity.

Realizing that the man who was essentially her

guide for the moment had kept on walking, she hurried to catch up with him.

She managed to reach him just as "Wayne" reached a bank of elevators located at the far end of the floor, a few feet beyond the registration desk.

Brennan nodded. "He has a suite near the top floor."

"And you?" she asked, not really sure what had prompted her to ask, other than she was attempting to live up to the image of a madam she was creating. "What do you have?"

An elevator car's door slid soundlessly open in front of them.

Brennan looked at her pointedly as they walked into the empty elevator car. He pressed number 30. "An itch I can't scratch—yet."

Was he actually putting her on notice, she wondered, stunned. "Saving yourself for Miss Right?" Tiana deadpanned.

The spontaneous laugh was deep and rich and all-encompassing within the small space. And, if she allowed it, it was also hypnotic in its own compelling way. Tiana did what she could to block the effects. Beyond his being good-looking, she knew nothing about the man. He could be a homicidal maniac for all she knew, even though her gut told her that he most likely wasn't.

"There's no such thing as 'Miss Right,'" Brennan told her.

"How do you know?" she asked, deciding to give him a hard time. "Just because you haven't encountered her yet doesn't mean she's not just around the next corner." As far as she was concerned, there were a great many "Miss Rights" out there. The main problem was that there were no "Mr. Rights" to receive them.

Numbers flashed by as they passed each floor. Brennan stared at his companion as if she'd lost her mind. "Never met a madam who was into fairy tales. How long did you say you were in this business?"

"It feels like all my life," she responded, infusing just the right amount of weariness into her voice.

They got out and he led the way down a winding hallway to a recessed door that appeared to be removed from the other rooms. This was clearly a suite among suites. Whoever this man was, Tiana thought, he certainly knew how to enjoy the fruits of his labors.

"Any word of advice?" she heard herself asking the tall man beside her.

She had to be crazy, but there was just the tiniest part of her that trusted this man—which on the face of it was nothing if not a foolhardy move on her part. Other than not really knowing this man from Adam, she realized again that she could very well be allying herself with a stone-cold killer. She had no way of knowing who or what he was. Why she should feel that she could trust him was a concept that was completely beyond her.

Since when had she turned into a trusting soul where men were concerned? a small voice in her head asked. She had no answer.

"Yeah," Brennan told her after a beat during which time he appeared to be weighing the pros and cons of answering her question at all, much less truthfully.

She might, after all, be trying to trap him. For all he knew, she was allied with Roland and had been sent to test him.

Maybe he was crazy, but he decided to take his chances—up to a point.

"Don't let your guard down around Roland for a second. He's a narcissist, but he's the type who wouldn't think twice about slitting your throat if he thinks you're lying to him—or if he believes that you went against him."

"Doesn't sound like he's going to be winning any Mister Nice Guy awards anytime soon," she quipped drolly.

"That's not his bottom line, no," Brennan agreed. He knocked on the door and it opened immediately.

A veritable giant of a man was standing in the doorway, blocking any access to the suite. She guessed he had to be about six foot six at the very least and he looked as though he weighed more than the two of them combined—perhaps even with Janie thrown into the mix. The seams on the suit he was wearing appeared to be stretched to the limit.

"Bodyguard?" she asked Brennan.

"More like all-around everything guard," he answered, never taking his eyes off the man.

The giant with the close-cropped blond hair regarded her through slits where his eyes should have been. The extra fat he was carrying in his face had all but crowded out his eyes, giving him a permanent squint that made the man's face look more ominous and menacing than it already did.

Recognition was evident in his eyes when he looked at her companion and he allowed the man to pass, but as she began to follow, he placed one hand against her upper torso, holding her back.

"Just him," he rumbled, his face unsmiling.

Brennan didn't attempt to remove the bodyguard's hand because it would be like trying to move a tree trunk. There was no pitting his strength against the giant's outright.

Instead, he looked at the man authoritatively and said, "She's with me. It's okay."

The bodyguard appeared to roll the matter over in his head; then he dropped his hand and inclined his head, as if to say she was allowed to pass. This time.

Swallowing the heart that had climbed up to her throat, Tiana glared at the bodyguard and told him in a voice filled with barely suppressed fury, "Don't you *ever* lay a hand on me again without an invitation."

Both men looked surprised at the bravado erupting from such a small, compact source. Brennan allowed a smile to slip over his lips.

"Pretty gutsy of you," he commented as they moved farther into the suite. "You do realize that he could easily have broken you in half like a twig without even half trying."

"I realize," she answered, her voice giving away nothing. She was silently relieved that it didn't crack and give her away.

The suite, she thought as she got a better look at it, was huge. Bigger than some houses. Definitely larger than the house where she and Janie had grown up. Business had to be very good.

The thought made her sick to her stomach. She wished she could take the man out right now, bring down his operation. But arresting Roland wouldn't get her anywhere. She needed tangible evidence.

"Should I be dropping bread crumbs?" she asked the man in front of her.

They had taken a couple of twists and turns within the suite and she was trying to commit each step to memory, but she really didn't like leaving anything to chance in case a quick getaway was necessary. The size of the place was overwhelming.

"Don't worry, I'll take you back," Brennan promised in a soothing voice.

She looked at him. He was acting as if they were on some ordinary stroll through the park instead of walking through a very sick bastard's temporary living accommodations.

"Why should I believe you?" she asked.

That was a simple enough question to answer. "Because you have no choice."

He was right and she hated him for it. Hated the fact that once again, everything was all on her shoulders and she had no one to look to, no one to trust or share the burden with. Her sister's life depended on what she did here.

If it's not already too late, a small, nagging voice whispered in her head. She clenched her hands at her sides as she blocked the voice.

Instead, she made a silent pledge—not her first—to

her sister. *Hang in there, Janie. No matter what, hang in there. I'll find you. I swear I'll find you.*

They entered what looked to be a sitting room. It was decorated entirely in stark white, which made the room appear twice as large. The only color in the immediate area was provided by the two men on the opposite sides of the room and the man in the middle who they were obviously paid to protect.

The deeply tanned guards appeared as if they were interchangeable, somewhat smaller versions of the guard at the front door. Both men were wearing dark navy blue suits, white shirts and dark ties. Each had a telltale bulge beneath his jacket, which Tiana assumed was caused by their not-so-concealed weapons.

The suits had to be specially tailored, she guessed, because the twin guards, like the man at the front door, were hulks in their own right.

The man in the center, looking out on the terrace with his back to them, was a great deal smaller height-wise. But he was far more imposing when he turned around to face them. While the guards were a compilation of sheer muscle and brute strength, the thin, dark-haired man had an aura of intelligent evil about him.

His eyes, as they passed over them—or accurately, over her—were flat. They were eyes that might have belonged to a dead man for all the expression that they had in them—except that she was fairly certain this man missed *nothing.*

Granted she spent most of her time in the lab when she was at work, but she could definitely recognize evil when she saw it. And this was the worst example of evil she had ever seen. It took effort not to shiver in its presence.

"You brought me a gift?" Roland asked Brennan. Approaching Tiana, he circled around her slowly as if she were an inanimate object, like a painting or a vase that had been given to him.

"No, she was in the motel room when I got there. He's dead, by the way," Brennan told Roland. "The kid you wanted me to check on. He's dead."

"You?" Roland asked, his implication clear.

"No," Brennan answered, wondering if all this was part of an elaborate game. He was fairly certain that Roland had been the one to have the young man killed. "I didn't kill him. He was already dead when I got there."

Roland raised one perfectly sculpted eyebrow. "You?" he asked, turning toward Tiana.

She shook her head, hoping she could keep the charade up long enough to find her sister. "No, I found him that way. Someone got to him before I could."

"The whore has a mouth on her," Roland announced with a nod. It was difficult to say whether there was admiration in the man's voice or if what they were hearing was the calm before a storm.

Not taking any chances, Brennan remained alert. He knew that things could turn on the head of a pin at any moment.

"She also isn't a whore," Tiana informed him with a toss of her head that seductively sent her flame red hair over her shoulder.

The appearance of amusement in Roland's features increased. "Oh, really?"

"Really," she confirmed in a no-nonsense tone of voice.

"You brought along your girlfriend?" the man questioned, as if he believed the woman's disclaimer.

"Why don't you talk to me instead of him?" Tiana proposed, making her voice sound as arrogant as the man she was speaking to. "Especially since he doesn't speak for me because he doesn't know me."

"Is this true?" Roland asked, looking at Brennan. What the man was thinking was impossible to gauge.

Brennan had no choice but to tell the truth without knowing where that might lead. "I just met her in the motel room."

"All right, who are you?" There was an unspoken threat in the man's voice that forbade her to say anything but the truth. It went without saying that it would go badly for her if she lied.

She said the lines that she had been practicing ever since she'd asked for a leave of absence. "I go by Aphrodite Starling and I've come with a business proposition for you."

The cold, dead eyes never left her face. "I'm listening."

"I run an escort service of young ladies, emphasis on the word *young,*" she began. "Some of my girls have aged out, shall we say? I'm in the market for replacements. I need fresh talent. Word has it that you have fresh talent," she told him, forcing herself not to look away. If she did, she knew he would take it as some kind of weakness—or worse. She had to win him over and do it fast.

"I might," he said vaguely, as if they were talking about a tool she wanted to borrow from his garage.

She kept it conversational, as if he was her first stop, but not necessarily her only one.

"I'd be interested in seeing what you have, perhaps taking a few off your hands." She paused a moment before adding, "I'll pay you top dollar."

The man appeared to only be vaguely interested, but she knew that had to be an act. Men like him were only in it for the money and they wanted as much as they could get their hands on as fast as they could get it.

"I'd like to see the color of your money," he told her.

She had a counterrequest. "I'd like to see the nature of your girls."

He laughed, shaking his head. "Not so fast. I don't even know who you are."

"And you won't," she told him matter-of-factly. "I don't broadcast my organization. Staying under the radar is how I survive. Word of mouth in a very small, elite, tight circle does all the advertising for me that I need. Once I'm confident that you can deliver—and that you're not just out to steal my money—I'll give you references and you can have me checked out to your heart's content."

"That sounds fair," he allowed, then added, "But I'll have to think about it. It doesn't pay to be trusting. You understand that?"

"Oh, perfectly." *Because I trust you as far as I can throw you,* she told the unsavory man silently. Still, what she thought of him didn't really matter. He had her sister, of that she was fairly certain. That gave him all the cards to hold. She just had her bluff, nothing more.

"I have photographs I can show you," Roland was telling her. "You can make your choices from them."

"Photographs can be easily doctored," she told him with just a hint of contempt in her voice. "When can I see the girls in person so I can make my choices?" she countered.

"My, my, such eagerness," Roland said with a laugh that had no humor in it whatsoever. "All in due time, my dear, all in due time."

Okay, if he wanted to play word games, she'd play along. Anything to gain his confidence—as far as it went. "I heard that time was scarce and that you and your 'people' would be leaving the country very soon."

He sneered at her gullibility—or at least that was his inference. "Don't believe everything you hear."

"Then you're not leaving soon?" she asked, watching his eyes for some sort of a sign that would give him away one way or another. When he didn't answer, she looked to the man who had brought her here for a confirmation or denial.

"Don't look at him," Roland warned sharply. "He doesn't have an answer to that any more than you do. You see, I do believe in equality. You will both be kept in the dark until such time as I feel you need to be enlightened. Not a moment sooner," he told her.

"All right, then, for the time being, I'll look at those photographs you have." The moment the words were out of her mouth, she knew it wasn't even going to be that easy—seeing a photograph of Janie wouldn't confirm that she was still alive. But she had to try even though she knew she was playing right into his hands. Maybe she could use that, she told herself. Use that to win the miserable human being over.

It was a long shot, but right now she didn't have anything else.

"Tomorrow," he said. "Come back tomorrow and perhaps I'll let you look at them then."

She played along and looked confused even though in her heart, she knew that the man was enjoying asserting his power.

"You just offered to show those photographs to me now," she protested, delivering just a part of the frustration she was beginning to feel building up inside her.

"I changed my mind. Women aren't the only ones with that prerogative, you know." The smile on his face indicated just how pleased he was with himself. "Give one of my men a cell number where you can be reached and I'll call if and when I want to see you again. You can go," he commanded like the tyrant he aspired to be within this growing organization, dismissing her with a wave of his hand.

Inwardly, Tiana was seething, but she couldn't afford to indulge herself and show it. Somehow, exercising supreme control, she managed to keep her feelings under wraps.

"Tomorrow, then," Tiana said to him as civilly as she could.

"Tomorrow," Roland said with a smirk. "Or the next day."

She turned on her heel and began to walk away. It was either that or lose all control and strangle the pompous ass.

When Brennan fell into place beside her, she looked at him almost accusingly. "I can find my way out of here without your help."

"I'm your ride, remember?" he reminded her cheerfully.

Roland, apparently, hadn't heard him say it. "Where are you going?" he demanded, eying Brennan, as if outraged that he'd leave without being dismissed.

"I'm taking her back to her car," Brennan answered. "I drove her here, thinking it was better if she didn't have a way to leave from the hotel unless you wanted her to leave."

Roland appeared rather impatient for a second, then shrugged.

"Not half-bad thinking. All right, be quick about it—and then come back. I want details from you about that motel room and then I might have another assignment for you. See if you're worth my time," he said loftily. "So whatever you're going to do," he ordered, and it was clear he wasn't referring to just a simple drop-off and delivery, "make sure you do it fast."

"I'll see what I can do to move things along," Brennan replied respectfully, playing up to the man because there were a great many lives at stake if he played the game correctly and well.

He was well aware that the woman beside him—who in his opinion remained an enigma—clearly had contempt in her eyes when she looked at him.

Chapter 5

Tiana waited until they were not just clear of the suite, but of the actual floor as well before she spoke again.

"Exactly what are you to him?" she asked as the elevator brought them back down to the hotel's ground floor.

He laughed shortly. In the two weeks since he'd wormed his way into Roland's inner circle, he'd been carefully walking on egg shells, every fiber of his being alert and watching for any telltale signs that he was in imminent danger. This while keeping his eyes and ears open, absorbing any information that might be available. He had yet to learn where the girls were being kept, but he was working on it.

So far, for some unknown reason, the man who made his mark in sex trafficking minors had taken a liking to him. But he knew that could easily change in a heartbeat—which was just the amount of time it took for his status to go from living to dead.

"Probably annoying," he guessed. There was no advantage to telling this woman that he and Roland got along. He never bragged about or called undue attention to a situation.

At the very least, that in itself might be inviting trouble.

"Very funny," she commented. "I mean in the scheme of things."

He shrugged. "I came here to fill an order, same as you."

The elevator stopped on the first floor and they got out, making their way out of the hotel to the self-parking lot across the street.

"If that's true, why does he treat you like an underling?" she asked.

He took that to mean she was asking why there appeared to be a certain lack of respect when Roland spoke to him. He saw no point in telling her that Roland had liked his style and said he could use someone of intelligence in his organization—after a trial internship—God, did that sound ludicrous or what?

"The man didn't exactly use kid gloves dealing with you, either," he pointed out. "And he has no reason to. He's in the catbird seat."

After buckling up once she was inside his sedan, she waited until he got in on his side and then asked, "Was I sensing some definite tension between you and the Hulk twins, or was that just my overactive imagination?"

Cutting around the vehicle in front of him, Brennan peeled out of the lot and hit the main road. "More like your astute ability to pick up on unique vibes," he told her. There was no harm in tossing her a small bone, and it might appease her enough to get her to stop asking questions. "My first encounter with the ugly twins, they wanted to keep me out of Roland's inner sanctum. I had different ideas." He flashed her a quick smile as they came to a stop at a red light. "My side won."

"Your side," she repeated. Did this man have a partner she hadn't met yet, someone she should be on her guard against? She had no way of finding out except to ask. "Who else is on your side?"

"As far as I know, I'm the only one on my side. If you'd like to join up," he told her, "there just happens to be a fresh opening."

He was leading her around in circles, trying to confuse her, she thought. "But Roland just said he had an assignment for you after you drop me off. Isn't that something a boss says to his henchman?" she asked pointedly.

"It is," he agreed. "Roland fancies himself everyone's boss. And he also wants to make sure that whoever he's dealing with has something to lose if his ring is ever exposed or brought down."

She could see that happening. "If you're afraid of going to jail along with him, then maybe you'll be careful not to run your mouth off or talk to the wrong people," she filled in.

He nodded. "Give the lady a prize. You catch on fast," he told her.

"Not exactly rocket science," Tiana pointed out.

Especially for someone who had been dealing with criminals by proxy the way she had. Granted she didn't go out in the field, but she read reports and tracked down evidence to nail criminals and put them away.

She studied his profile for a moment, trying to find another way to get the information she both needed and desperately sought. "So you're interested in acquiring some of the girls he has?"

"I am."

"Have you gotten to see any of them?" She did her best to make it sound as if she were just having a regular conversation, not holding her breath, waiting for his answer.

"Just some assorted photos." His gaze revealed a flicker of suspicion toward her. "He has me on ice, same as you."

"You got to see photographs," she pointed out. "That is *not* same as me."

"I'm a little closer to the finish line than you are," he told her. And also, the man, no doubt, had decided he wanted to toy with her first. And because he was undoubtedly having her checked out, just as he had him, Brennan thought. His identity had been fabricated by the chief of Ds' daughter–in-law, so there were no holes. He wondered if this woman's identity was just as airtight—or if she would wind up being in trouble.

Not your concern. You're not here to rescue her. You're saving kidnap victims, remember?

"So, what do the girls in the photographs look like?" she asked.

He heard the tension in her voice, even though she was doing her best to hide it. What was that all about?

"Like girls," he told her. "Young girls," he added, emphasizing the word *young*.

That didn't help her any, didn't get her any closer to finding Janie. "I mean, are they blondes, brunettes, redheads?"

"Yeah, they are," he answered, studying her as he answered her question. He saw impatience crease her forehead. "All three," he added. "Why? Do your clients have a 'type' as well as an age requirement?" he asked.

She paused for a moment, then replied, "Strawberry blondes."

Janie was a strawberry blonde and it was driving her crazy that she couldn't find out whether or not her sister was even here. All this role-playing, all this spinning of wheels and it could all be for nothing.

Maybe Janie had managed to get away from Wayne before he'd come here. Or maybe she escaped while whoever it was that had killed Wayne was busy eliminating him.

Tiana bit her lower lip, knowing she was clutching at straws.

"Like you?" he asked, turning down the next block.

"Blonder," she automatically corrected, then added, "I've got red hair, not strawberry blonde."

"Now that I think of it, there were a couple of

those in the batch Roland let me look at. Strawberry blondes," he elaborated in case she thought he was referring to redheads. "How many are you looking for?"

She did her best to sound businesslike, not wanting to arouse any undue suspicions on his part. For all she knew, everything he'd told her was a lie and he was working for Roland and charged with checking her out firsthand.

"That all depends on what they look like in person. As many as Roland currently has to start with."

A thought occurred to her as she was talking to the man she was forced to interact with. She had brought a photograph of Janie to show around. She needed to find out if Wayne had brought her sister with him to the motel or if Janie had become Roland's "property" before then.

Think like a CSI, not like a sister, Tiana ordered herself. It was her only hope and the best course of action, but that didn't mean that it was easy.

She needed to gather together as much information as she could. Right now, until it started to make more sense, everything she could get her hands on was a potential piece of the puzzle. She was aware that there were bound to be pieces that didn't fit, that didn't belong to the puzzle at all, but she wouldn't know that until she'd examined each piece to see what, if anything, it had to offer.

By this time, anxious to get started, she was practically sitting on the edge of her seat despite the seat belt that was all but cutting her in half as it continued to restrain her.

"I am taking you back to your car," he told her after a couple of minutes of silence had lapsed between them.

She slanted an impatient glance in his direction. Why was he saying that? Was he trying to divert her attention from something? If that was the case, she hadn't a clue what it could be.

"I know that."

"You sure?" he asked.

Her body language told him that something else was going on, but he knew she wasn't about to volunteer anything. Maybe if he made a right guess, she might give herself away for a split second. It was all he had to work with.

It occurred to him again that she could be exactly what she claimed to be, but something in his gut said she was only playing at this "madam" thing until it got her the goal she had her sights on. Whatever the hell that turned out to be.

"The way you're sitting on the edge of your seat, you look like you're going to take flight the second I stop the car."

"Just your imagination," she said, dismissing his question.

"I don't have one," he said simple.

"Everyone has one," she told him. "You just don't realize it."

He took a corner and she could see the motel up ahead on the right. He had begun to signal his intention to make a right turn in order to enter the parking lot when she told him, "You can stop the car right here. I can walk the rest of the way to my car."

"I figured I'd give you door-to-door service," he quipped.

"No need," she said, already unbuckling her seat belt.

He anticipated her next move. This was one bull-headed woman. "I guess I'd better stop before you leap out of the car," Brennan said, pulling the sedan over to the side.

The second he did, he saw her get out. He hadn't even have time to turn his engine off.

"Thanks," she tossed over her shoulder. "See you." And with that, she pushed the passenger door closed and hurried up the block to the rear lot. She'd left her vehicle parked there.

But rather than get into it once she reached it, Tiana deliberately paused for a moment beside it, then got in. Her key was in her hand, but it never entered the ignition. Instead, she did a mental countdown.

Waiting.

Then, when she was satisfied that Wayne had driven by and was on his way back to the flesh peddler they had just left, Tiana got out of her car and hurried into the motel's rental office.

The manager, a slight man whose sparse hair was a shade of bootblack that looked so lifelessly artificial, it screamed *hair dye* from a block away, had his eyes glued to a flat-screen that looked far too expensive for the man to own.

She cleared her throat to get his attention. When she

failed, she cleared her throat a second time, a great deal more loudly this time. It had the same results. Finally, she said in a loud voice, "Excuse me."

Instead of turning around and giving her his attention, the small man held up his right index finger, as if that would put her on hold until he was ready to deal with her.

"Be with you in a minute," he muttered. "Wait for a commercial."

"All right," she retorted, thinking that the man might be more receptive if she played along and let him watch what looked to her to be a brain-numbing display of pyrotechnics thinly disguised as a story.

But when the commercial break came a couple of minutes later, the motel manager quickly clicked his remote to bring him to another channel.

"Excuse me," she tried again only to have him hold up his index finger the way he had done the first time and repeat the same comment he'd already said a couple of minutes earlier. "Wait for a commercial."

She drew out her weapon and said in a very even voice, "Unless you want me to shoot a hole in the middle of that damn flat-screen, you'll talk to me now."

The manager glanced contemptuously at her, thinking she was merely issuing a baseless threat. The second he saw the gun in her hand, he quickly turned completely around to face her, his hands raised high over his head. "The cashbox only has credit card receipts in it—"

"I'm not after your money," she retorted. "All I want are a few answers."

"Sure, anything you say, just please don't shoot," he begged.

Still holding the weapon for insurance, Tiana pulled out the photograph she'd put in her pocket. "Have you seen this girl?" she asked.

The manager squinted myopically at the photograph. Pipe-cleaner-thin shoulders rose and fell. "I might have," he said, then added a very shaky "Maybe."

"You either did or you didn't," Tiana ground out. "She would have been here in the last couple of days. Checking into a room with the guy you have in room thirteen," she added.

The manager's eyes widened, further perpetuating the impression that his eyes resembled loose brown marbles. He never took them off her weapon.

"He came in alone," he told her, barely refraining from stuttering. "I never saw no girl with him. Maybe she coulda been in his car, but I never looked. Why don't you go and ask him?" he suggested nervously.

The manager's suggestion, added to the fact that there were no police cars converging in the immediate vicinity and equally important, there was no yellow tape stretched across the motel door, barring entrance, told her that no one had discovered Wayne's body yet.

But it couldn't be that much longer.

"Take another look," she urged, pushing the photograph toward him on the dusty, scarred desk until it was right in front of him. "You're sure you haven't seen her anywhere? Not in the parking lot or going to the ice machine?"

"I don't know," the man whined. "People come and go here and they don't like being noticed, so I make it my business not to look directly at them if I can help it. They pay their bill, that makes them okay. They don't pay, then I notice them."

There was some sort of action taking place on the show he had flipped to just before she had commandeered his attention. Tiana could see that his focus was already divided between talking to her and trying to make out what was happening on the TV screen.

Her mind scrambled around for anything else she could ask the manager; anything that could actually *help* find Janie and not just take her off on another wild goose chase.

"How far in advance did he pay for the room?" she asked.

It was evident by the expression on the manager's face that his brain, limited at best, had ceased functioning altogether.

"Who?" he asked.

"The man in room thirteen," she snapped. This man needed to borrow twelve IQ points to qualify being labeled a moron, she thought angrily.

He began to wave a dismissive hand in her direction, his eyes darting back to the TV. "I'm not supposed to give out that—"

"How far in advance did he pay for the room?" she repeated, resting her hand on the hilt of the weapon she'd tucked into the front of her waistband.

Glancing in her direction, the manager was thrown into instant terror again and gave up the stance he'd taken, which had been a wavering one at that. It was clear that he wasn't about to protect *anyone* if it meant he was going to get hurt in the process.

"I'll look, I'll look," the little man cried, scrolling through the data on his small computer screen. "Here he is, right there," he practically sobbed, jabbing at the screen with his broken fingernail. "He's checking out tomorrow," he announced, reading what was on the monitor.

Finished, his head bobbed up immediately and he watched her fearfully. "Is that what you needed to know?" he asked, swallowing. His Adam's apple moved up and down as if it were precariously tied to a string and was all set to dance.

No, it wasn't, she thought. What she needed to know was where Wayne had left her sister and what had happened to her since then.

Wayne's checkout date told her that he expected to have business wrapped up by tomorrow.

And, in a way, she supposed he was right. Just not in the way he'd expected. But Wayne was *not* her concern. Her sister was.

"Thanks for your help," she said sarcastically to the manager. She put her hand in her pocket and the man cringed and ducked, obviously expecting her to make a grab for the weapon in her waistband and discharge it in his direction.

His eyes almost fell out when she threw a twenty down on the counter in payment for his information.

Grabbing the bill as if he were afraid it would suddenly sprout legs and walk away, the motel manager appeared slightly less tense. He clutched the twenty and raised his voice, calling after her as she opened the door to leave.

"Anything else you need to know?" he asked, obviously hoping for more money to be thrown his way.

"Nothing you can help me with," Tiana retorted, sparing him a last withering look.

The man had the common sense to step back, as if he knew that he had come precariously close to paying for something he had no way of knowing about.

"Good luck finding her," he added just as the door closed.

Even as the words registered, she could feel her heart sinking just a little further as she fought off a hopelessness that threatened to completely consume her whole.

No, damn it, you're not letting it get to you. You're made of stronger stuff than that. You know that, Tiana lectured herself sternly.

Later, after she found Janie and brought her home, after this whole dirty business was behind her, *then* she would have time to break down and sob—but not now. "Now" was for moving heaven and earth until she found her sister's trail.

With slightly renewed energy, Tiana got into her car and put the key in the ignition. But she hadn't even turned the key to start the engine when she became aware of someone walking up to the driver's-side window. The person tapped lightly against the glass.

Her heart rose in her throat before she realized that the person standing just outside her window was

"Bruce Wayne"—or whatever the hell he had decided to call himself now.

For a second, Tiana thought of gunning her engine and peeling out of the lot, but something kept her where she was. Besides, she wasn't much of an expert on cars, but she knew enough about them to know that his vehicle was a great deal faster than hers and once he got back behind the wheel, he'd catch up to her in no time flat.

And she had no other connection to finding her sister besides this man.

So instead, she remained where she was, rolled down her window and snapped, "What?"

"Find out anything useful?" Brennan asked mildly, as if this were just another everyday conversation they were about to engage in.

Chapter 6

It took a second for her heart to stop beating wildly. She hadn't even realized that the man who called himself Wayne was approaching her until he was literally at her window, tapping on the glass. At this point, he wasn't even supposed to be anywhere in the immediate vicinity.

So why was he?

"What are you doing here?" Tiana demanded. She hated being caught off guard like this.

He gave her an easygoing smile. "Standing next to your car, asking you a question."

She could feel her temper rising. The answer he'd given her was far too literal and she felt he was being condescending to her. Why was he playing games like this with her?

Just what *was* his game?

"You couldn't have gone to see Roland and come back in such a short amount of time," she pointed out, daring him to lie.

But he didn't. "No," he agreed, "I couldn't."

"So you never went," she concluded.

"Nope."

Once he'd cleared the lot, he had pulled over to the side and then seemed to wait for her car to leave the lot. When it didn't, he'd doubled back obviously to see what she was up to.

"Why are you following me?" she asked bluntly.

His mouth curved in a smile that would have, under possible other circumstances, curled her toes—or at least given her a lengthy pause. But right now he was the enemy, most likely tied in somehow to Janie's disappearance, and she needed to remember that—and keep her guard up at all time.

"Let's just say I have an inordinate amount of curiosity about certain things," he told her.

"And satisfying that curiosity—or hoping to—is worth running the risk to alienating Roland and irritating the hell out of him?" she asked. Tiana didn't believe him. It just didn't make any sense. Something else was up; she could *feel* it.

Brennan laughed. "I have a lot of money to spend. Roland likes to collect a lot of money. It'll work itself out," he promised her, dismissing her supposed concern. "So, did you find anything out?" he asked her again.

Since she sensed he was being far from truthful

with her, she was determined to return the favor and not volunteer a shred of any sort of information.

"About what?" she countered stubbornly.

"About what you came back to ask the motel manager about—" His eyes met hers and she could almost *feel* him penetrating her innermost thoughts. "That strawberry blonde you're trying to track down. Did he tell you anything?"

For a second, Tiana felt herself freeze inside. This man standing at her car window was so accurate in his assumptions, it was as if he'd found a way to hack into her brain. But that was just an illusion he was trying to create so that he could pump her for some *real* information.

She'd run across a psychic or two during her time with crime scene investigations and they all operated the same way. They were intuitive people who knew how to read others. They picked up on clues other people unintentionally gave off and they watched intently for any sort of "tells." If the person shifted or seemed suddenly more alert, or his eyes widened at the mention of something personal, then a correct guess had been made and he'd start to expand on that "guess."

This "Wayne" was just good at making guesses, that was all.

"I don't know what you're talking about," she said harshly. "I'm not looking for *a* strawberry blonde, I'm looking for *lots* of strawberry blondes because right now my clients have all expressed an interest in that 'type.' I've already told you that once. How many times do I have to say it?"

Instead of answering, he surprised her by rounding the hood of her car and opening the passenger door. Slipping into the seat, he fixed her with a look for a long moment before asking, "Who are you?"

Did he think he was going to wear her down by asking the same things over and over again? Well, he was going to be sorely disappointed if that's what he thought. "I already told you—"

"What you told me was a story." He glared at her sternly. "None of my contacts have ever heard of you."

Digging deeply into her bravado, she pretended to be on the verge of losing her temper with this man who might or might not be Roland's minion.

Whatever or whoever he really was, he was making her nervous in a very bad way.

"That's *because* I'm good at keeping under the radar. I told you that before, too."

"It was a lie then, and it's a lie now," he informed her. He'd done some very quick checking with Brenda while this so-called madam was inside the rental office, most likely intimidating the manager. Brenda found no information on this woman, which in turn was information in itself. "None of my contacts' contacts have heard of you, either—and *nobody's* that good at erasing their trail," he told her in case she was going to harp on that being-under-the-radar thing again.

Tiana raised her chin. "I am," she told him, never wavering.

He laughed softly to himself. The lady had guts, he'd give her that. She was trying to face him down when she had to know that if he so chose, he could easily have just eliminated her with a twist of his hand. Her neck was long and slender and a relatively easy target for someone with a short fuse and accustomed to taking matters into their own hands. Literally.

"Maybe you are at that," he conceded for the time being. He didn't want to waste any more time going around and around about this one point. He was positive she was just posing as a madam. The question remained as to why and if the answer would in any way impede his finding where the new "talent" was being kept and, just as important, who was actually calling the shots. He was fairly certain that it wasn't Roland—although there was an outside chance that he might be wrong about that.

"Where are you staying?" he asked, changing the subject.

"Where am I staying?" she repeated, trying to understand why he was asking.

Was he just interested in getting into her bed? Or was it so that he could eliminate her when her guard was down? Granted she'd decided that he didn't look like a killer, but then, a lot of killers didn't look as if they were capable of the deed.

"Yes, 'staying,'" he repeated, his expression unreadable. "As in a room with a bed, a shower, four walls, that kind of thing."

Maybe he *was* just interested in sex. She knew of several women who would have been more than willing to accommodate him and would probably have thought she was crazy for not jumping at the chance to encourage him. But there was no way this was going to go that route. "I'm not your type."

"No, you're not," he agreed purely for the sake of argument because, under different circumstances away from this job, she might very well be his type—at least for a night or two. The lady looked very capable of making intense sparks fly for a recreational couple of hours. Or days—and *not* because she was professing to be a madam. She was a knockout and her looks were a definite distraction, but he had a mission, his first in this new situation he and the rest of his family found themselves in.

Failure was less of an option now than it ever had been before.

Tiana stared at him. Had she just received a put-down? "Then why do you want to know where I'm staying?"

"In case I want to talk to you."

"I'll let you in on a little secret—that's why phones were invented."

Brennan slowly moved his head from side to side, dismissing her point. "Yeah, maybe, but I'm a face-to-face kind of guy. I like to see a person's eyes when I talk to her."

Suspicions rose again. Paranoia was becoming a way of life these past few days. She began to wonder if she was ever going to feel whole again—and on firm ground. "Why?"

"Because you can tell a lot about a person by looking into his eyes." Just the way he was looking into hers, he thought. Maybe he was crazy, but what he saw there told him that while she was definitely on some sort of mission or crusade, making arrangements for the purchase of new "merchandise" was not really part of it.

"Is that anything like reading a person's palm?" she mocked.

"Not even close," he replied with a perfectly straight face. "When a person lies, there's a very slight hesitation in her eyes."

"What about a career liar?" she challenged. "Like a politician."

Even there, a person could tell, he thought, *if* he knew what to look for. "The eyes shut down, which is just as good because you don't shut down unless you have something you want to hide."

"You can bend the facts like a pretzel to suit your purposes, can't you?" she asked.

It was a definite criticism—but he had one of his own for her. "And you run from the facts like an Artful Dodger. What's the matter, *Aphrodite?*" he asked. "What is there about the truth that scares you?"

"Nothing at all," she told him, her eyes flashing as she raised her chin defiantly again. It was a tug-of-war to get the upper hand and she refused to allow him to win out over her. But as for his initial question, she had a feeling that he would go on badgering her until she told him the truth. Either that or he would follow, which wasn't going to happen because she really didn't have anywhere to go. "And as for where I'm staying, I'm not."

It didn't take much to figure out what she was telling him. "You breezed into town and went straight to that motel to see the dead guy, is that it?"

She knew that things would go more smoothly for her if she mixed a bit of the truth into the tale she was fabricating, so she conceded to his summary. "Something like that."

He nodded, silently telling her that he believed what she was telling him. "Who was he to you?"

The key to everything right now, she thought in frustration. "Just a connection."

"To what?" he pressed, never taking his eyes off hers. And doing his best not to be mesmerized by them at the same time.

She shrugged, indicating that the answer was obvious. "To Roland apparently."

He sincerely doubted that she saw him in that kind of lofty capacity. "The kid in the motel room wasn't in your league," he pointed out.

"I wasn't planning on marrying him," she said, annoyed that he was picking apart every word she said. She'd always found these sorts of mind games wearying and of absolute no merit. She wasn't fond of chess in any sort of venue, especially when she felt that her opponent was trying to wear her down. "He had access to information I needed, so I went to see him. End of story."

He looked at her knowingly. He wasn't buying it. "But it isn't, is it? It's not the end of the story for you."

Okay, enough was enough, she thought. She'd been nice and played along, but now it was time to end this little charade, or philosophical dance. "If you're looking to wear me down, you're wasting your time—and mine. Now, if you don't mind, I'm hungry and I'd like to get something to eat, so—"

He cut her off and said in a far more hearty voice, "Sounds good to me."

She stared at him. The man was incorrigible. "That wasn't an invitation."

He smiled tolerantly. "Just an oversight on your part, I'm sure."

"No, I'm rather sure it wasn't," she responded firmly. "Now, if you don't mind—"

Again he interrupted her. "Not in the slightest." Before she could tell him to get out of her car, he hit her with a question out of the blue. "Are you familiar with the area?"

If she lied, he'd probably quiz her by dropping some establishment name on her that she'd never heard of. "No, I'm not—"

"Well, lucky for you," he said with an accommodating grin, "I am. There's this great little restaurant about four miles from here. They make a prime rib steak that makes you think you've died and gone to heaven."

She was pretty much at the end of her temper and she made no attempt to hide the fact. *Something* had to make this man back away. "I just want one that makes me think I'm dining alone."

The expression on his face testified that he didn't believe her. "Is that any way for someone named Aphrodite to act?"

"You mean picky about the company she keeps?"

Tiana guessed pointedly, refusing to give in. "Yes, I'm pretty certain that it is."

Rather than to back off, he kept trying to find a crack in her defenses. "C'mon, what's one meal going to hurt?" he coaxed.

Ordinarily, he would have backed off long before this. But there was more to this woman than met the eye, and he wanted his chance to find out what that "more" was. Since he had no way of knowing where the break would come from—the one that would allow him to gain access to the *real* inner world of these flesh peddlers, he couldn't leave any stone unturned, and right now she had to be the most attractive stone he had hopes of turning over, bar none.

"I'm thinking a lot," she told him, hoping to put him off. She might have known better.

"Maybe that's just the problem," he guessed.

"My thinking?" she asked incredulously. Just because he was probably used to women with the IQ of a carrot didn't mean that all women were like that, or were happier like that.

"Your *over*thinking," he corrected. Then he went back to coaxing for a positive response. "The restaurant will be crowded. There'll be a lot of people there. You'll be safe," he guaranteed.

"If you have to go out of your way to tell me I'll be safe, then I'm rather certain that I damn well won't be safe there—possibly not safe anywhere."

"I repeat, what can happen to you in a crowded restaurant? I'll even let you drive," he said, buckling up in the passenger seat and then raising his hands up like a prisoner with no options before him other than to give up defending his land or to defend it to the death. "That way you're in control," he told her cheerfully.

"Takes more than a steering wheel to be in charge," she informed him.

He inclined his head. "True," he agreed. "But it's a start."

Her stomach was really beginning to pinch her. She wasn't going to do Janie any good starving herself or allowing herself to become the embodiment of malnutrition, and she was having trouble remembering when she'd actually eaten last. Everything had been focused on coming down here and searching for her sister as soon as possible.

Now that her only viable connection to Janie was lying in a pool of his own blood, she had to find another lead.

"All right," she agreed grudgingly. "Where is this fantastic restaurant of yours?"

"If it were mine, you could eat there every night for free," he told her. He smiled like a chess champion making that final move that rendered his opponent completely neutralized, with no options open except to surrender. Mind games, she reminded herself. These were just mind games and all she had to do was stand firm. "You go down this block and make a left at the light. Head straight, then make another left turn where Ball intersects Fairview."

She nodded, turning on her ignition.

Following his directions, she made a second left

where he told her, then glanced at him, waiting for further instructions.

He obliged. "Two blocks from here, make a right."

"What's this restaurant called?" Sensing that they were getting close, she wanted to know what name she should be looking for.

"A Little Piece of Heaven."

"I didn't ask what the food tastes like," she told him pointedly. "I want to know the name."

"Both," he told her. "It's both." The exasperated look she shot him only succeeded in amusing him. "There it is, up ahead," he said, pointing it out.

The sign on top of the building proclaimed it to be A Little Piece of Heaven. Its appearance, however, negated that assessment, at least as far as looks went. The building was in serious disrepair and needed more than a little tender love and care to look respectable.

"It looks more like A Little Piece of Hovel," she said.

"Well, there you go," he said as if the restaurant were making his argument for him. "Looks can mislead you," Brennan concluded.

It was like being in the company of a book of useless platitudes and clichés. "If you say anything further along the lines of looks can be deceiving, I promise you'll live to regret it."

She could feel his eyes on her, taking measure, reducing her to what, she wasn't sure, but it had to be something he dealt with on a regular basis.

She parked her car and got out. He was right there

beside her. They walked toward the restaurant's front entrance.

"I doubt very much if I'll regret any of this," he told her.

She sighed and shook her head as they approached the restaurant in question. "How long did you have to practice before this smooth way of talking came naturally to you?"

"No practice. Some things you're just born with— like red hair," he said, pausing before the massive wooden front door and feathering a strand of her hair through his fingers.

She automatically pulled it out of his fingers.

There was something far too personal about the way he'd touched her hair. The intimate action seemed to strip her of her self-assurance, both the one she clung to and the one she was careful to project.

Wayne made her feel as if she were completely transparent—but she wasn't, she told herself. That was just his way of undermining her.

She was her own person and she was very aware of what she was doing here—and what would happen if she wasn't successful.

This man was not just a sexy smile and a swagger, she told herself. He could very well be the key to finding her sister. At the very least, she had a feeling—one that she couldn't substantiate but it was still there— that Wayne would keep her safe if it came down to needing that.

Or maybe she was just losing the ability to be sensible.

"Let's just keep this strictly business," she told him.

"Never crossed my mind to keep it anything else," he assured her, spreading his hands in what amounted to an innocent gesture.

"I might look gullible, but I'm not," she told him pointedly. "And even if I were somewhat gullible," she conceded, "*nobody's* that gullible," she added, referring to his comment that he hadn't thought about trying to make things personal between them.

Cocking his head, he looked at her quizzically. "I don't follow you."

"Your 'innocent' act isn't working," she informed him—needlessly in her opinion.

The man beside her laughed softly, the sound weaving itself under her skin despite the din in the restaurant that they entered. "I haven't been 'innocent' since I turned five years old."

"Now, *that* I can readily believe," she told him.

He smiled in return, then slipped his arm through hers and guided her, not entirely against her will, toward the hostess table.

The slender young woman with the straight dark brown hair looked at them and asked, "Two?"

Brennan nodded, confirming her assumption. "Two."

Tiana had no idea why that number sounded so exceedingly intimate to her, but it did.

As she walked behind the hostess and half a step ahead of Wayne, she did her best to shake herself free of that feeling.

It refused to leave.

Chapter 7

Brennan waited until the hostess had shown them to a booth, handed them their menus and discreetly withdrawn before saying anything to this woman who aroused his curiosity and stirred his imagination.

Deciding to go along with the persona she was projecting, he asked her, "So, how did you happen to get into this line of work?"

Tiana studied the menu for a moment. The description was straightforward, lacking in effusive adjectives. The selection itself was limited, but the prices were reasonable. Maybe that was the real draw here, she mused. It certainly wasn't the ambience.

Glancing up for half a second, she murmured, "I could ask you the same thing," before looking over the dessert section of the menu. That was even more limited.

"You can, but I asked first." Brennan grinned when she looked up at him, a trace of impatience furrowing her brow. "I'll show you mine if you show me yours," he proposed.

"What are you asking, to hear my life story?"

"At least the abbreviated version."

Conversation was curtailed briefly as a waitress—apparently the only one working the floor from the looks of it—came to take their order. They both ordered the same thing—prime rib—except that his was medium and hers wasn't. She liked her steak just barely dead.

And when the woman went to place their orders, Tiana looked at the man sitting across from her and resumed their conversation, picking up the threads exactly where they were dropped.

"Why?"

Brennan looked almost amused. "You ask that a lot," he noted.

"I suppose I do," she allowed. "But there's a reason for that. Because you ask a lot of questions," she pointed out.

"Fair enough." He paused as the waitress arrived with his drink—and her glass of water. "I was just wondering why someone who looks as if she's got a lot going for her wouldn't try to do something more legitimate," Brennan said, making his point as the young server wove her way to another table.

Tiana stared into the glass of water as she shrugged. "Maybe I'm just lazy and this comes easy."

"No, it doesn't," he countered. She looked up at him and he gave her an explanation. "If you were lazy, you wouldn't have put together an 'escort' service," he pointed out.

She wasn't about to argue any point. She'd found that being nebulous and vague was a far better course to take. And for the time being, what was easiest for her was to take her own background and embellish on it.

"Okay. Maybe I had a mother who decided to run out on me when I was ten, leaving me with a father who was a cop and brought new meaning to the word *strict*."

As she spoke, she could practically see her father in front of her. She supposed that in his own way, he'd tried, but he was short on patience and long on anger. And she looked a great deal like her mother, so he took his anger out on her. Whatever was left over spilled out on Janie.

Her sister was more fragile, while she was the tougher of the two. She did what she could to get him to take things out on her rather than Janie. That had left scars.

Her mouth twisted as the dark memories rose before her. There were times during those days when she was sure she wasn't going to survive. And yet she had. Which made her stronger than she had initially thought.

"A father," she continued, "who made me account

for every minute of my life when I was out of the house, even if it was just in school." The laugh was short and totally devoid of humor, just as her life had been back then. "Maybe the escort service is my way of rebelling and putting him in his place."

"Is it?" Brennan asked, his eyes on hers.

It seemed to her that there was no one else in the restaurant except for the two of them despite the fact that the handful of tables and booth in the small establishment were all taken.

Tiana had deliberately dipped into her own past and used what was there as a starting point in order to weave an acceptable story for this man with his endless questions. It was only meant to be a jumping-off point, and she hadn't meant to go that deeply into her life or jar the memories she had. It had taken her a long while to pack them all neatly away.

But ever since Janie had disappeared, the memories had found their way back up to the surface, bobbing and weaving before her like a taunting reminder.

To show you what you've accomplished, what you've risen above, not who you were, she silently insisted.

"Maybe," was all she would say on the subject. Tiana was more than ready to turn the tables on this snoop. Let *him* answer some questions for a change. "Isn't it about time you did a little sharing of your own?" she asked, prodding him.

He obliged her, ready for a capsulated version of his own upbringing, which had been average, but the one thing he'd never lacked for was love, something he had a feeling this woman he was talking to couldn't say.

As he began to open his mouth, the waitress returned with their dinners. "Careful, they're hot," she warned needlessly, then made herself scarce, leaving a parting word: "Enjoy."

Tiana looked at him pointedly, obviously waiting for him to live up to his side of the bargain.

"Can't blame what I do on my childhood, which, looking back, was pretty good—especially compared to yours," he added. "I just kind of fell into this. It came easy, so I stayed. No traumatic reason," he confessed, "I just like money and this came easy. No years of studying, no climbing my way up some corporate ladder, no getting stabbed in the back by some over-eager toady."

Tiana laughed harshly as she took a sip from the water glass before her. "You make it sound like a dream come true."

"Well, at least somebody's dream," he conceded. Then he nodded at the glass of water she'd just set down again. "You sure you wouldn't rather have something with a kick to it?"

"I'm sure," she replied firmly.

"A madam who doesn't drink." He rolled the concept over in his mind. "That doesn't sound quite right," he observed, although he had to admit that she struck him as someone who didn't care about other people's opinions about what she did.

"I like keeping a clear head," she told him. "That's how I stay one step ahead of the competition and anyone who wants to work their way up *my* corporate ladder," she said, playing his words back to him.

Brennan nodded and set down the drink he'd ordered—whiskey, neat. He'd only taken a couple of sips himself. If she wasn't drinking, then he didn't have to in order to play his part.

"You might be onto something," he conceded, then asked completely out of the blue, "What do you think of Roland?"

"What should I think of him?"

He wasn't fishing for something deep. "Just that. You know, Venus—you don't mind if I call you that, do you? It the Roman version of your name and it's less of a mouthful than Aphrodite."

She shrugged. "Whatever makes you happy," she allowed, then saw the look on his face. She'd walked right into that one, she told herself. "Within reason," Tiana specified.

Brennan laughed, amused. "Nice save. What I started to say was that not everything is a test or needs to be examined seven ways from sundown before you answer. I just wondered if you had the same impression I did." He saw her raise a quizzical eyebrow and obliged by giving her his own opinion first. "That he was living large but that he wasn't the top of the totem pole."

"You mean that he's taking orders from someone else," she said, putting it into other, simpler words.

He nodded. "That's what I mean."

"Probably." She gave him her take on the way things were set up within this organization. "There're the recruiters who bring in the talent any way they can, like the kid in the motel room," she bit off contemptuously. "There's the middleman or -woman who keeps track of what's going on and houses the 'talent' until such time as the girls are either shipped out, sold or rejected, and there's someone at the head of all this who makes a nice living off everybody else's efforts. He gets the lion's share of the money, which he feels entitled to because he put up the original seed money and he also greases whatever palms need greasing and makes sure the right people are looking the other way so that the flow of this particular 'traffic' isn't impeded." She concluded by taking another long sip of water to keep from gagging on her words. The scenario she'd outlined made her sick when she gave any real thought to it.

"I'm impressed. You know this business pretty well."

For a second, she allowed herself to bask in the unintended compliment. She had made it her business to take a huge crash course in the way these sleazy, sickening organizations were run when the rumors that there were flesh peddlers looking for fresh slaves began surfacing.

Janie's worthless boyfriend's roommate had indirectly been her initial source of direct information. When she'd come looking for Wayne, Jack, his roommate, told her he'd kicked Wayne out when he discovered that he was mixed up in finding girls who could be easily talked into voluntarily going into the life because of the "rewards" that waited for them down the line: money, expensive clothes, jewelry.

She'd shown the former roommate Janie's picture

and he had recognized her sister as being Wayne's newest girlfriend. She'd quickly filled in the gaps in her education with information she picked up from other police officers.

"Oh, good," she cracked in response to "Wayne's" compliment. "Now I can die happy."

He paused for a moment, as if considering her comment, then changed topics entirely. "So, have you given any thought to where you are staying after we leave here?"

Didn't take a rocket scientist to see where this was going. "Let me guess, you're going to offer me your room to crash in— You've got a room, right? Or do you keep an apartment here?" That was the only unknown in this, she felt.

"I travel light. It's a room," he answered. "Actually, it's more like two rooms. A bedroom and a sitting area." He felt that might just come in handy. And now, apparently, it actually might. "And if I did offer, would you take me up on it?"

"'Come into my parlor, said the spider to the fly.'" Her mouth curved knowingly. "I wasn't born yesterday, 'Wayne.' Or the day before," she added, waiting to hear his answer, her eyes on his. He didn't strike her as someone who gave up easily, but then again, this was about far more than just a one-night stand.

"Didn't mean to imply that I thought you were," he told her. "Just trying to be friendly—and helpful."

"Is that what you call it now?" she mocked with a humorless laugh. "I'll find my own accommodations, thanks."

He shrugged, pushing his empty plate away. "Fine with me. I just thought it might be easier for both of us if we joined forces."

Just what was "Wayne" up to? she wondered. "Easier how?"

He gave her the most logical scenario. One that, he was certain, had probably occurred to her already. "Well, Roland's got all that muscle behind him. What's to stop him from taking our money and not delivering the merchandise?"

She hated that her sister—and girls like her—were considered nothing more than chattel. "And the two of us together would be formidable enough to keep him from doing that?" The very idea was laughable.

"Two are better than one," Brennan pointed out. "And they just might not be expecting this alliance. This way, if one of us gets to find out where the girls are being kept, that one can let the other know. If nothing else," he went on, "that way we can make the best selections rather than just be forced to take what he decides to sell us. This alliance isn't about hooking up, it's about strictly business." Having laid out his pitch, he backed off. He didn't want her thinking he was pushing this too hard. "But hey, it's up to you," he concluded with a shrug.

"Strictly business?" she repeated. Her tone indicated that she was challenging him more than she was just asking a question.

"Yeah, strictly business. Like I said, I've got a bedroom and a sitting room. Bedroom's got a door. You can take that. I'll take the couch." It couldn't get any more chaste sounding than that, he thought. And if he had the couch, she had to pass him before she reached the door. He slept lightly enough to hear a leaf fall on a rug. There was no way she was going to make a getaway without his knowing it.

Her eyes held his, utilizing his trick on him. "You'd do that for me?"

He nodded. "Yeah."

She wasn't buying it. There had to be something she was missing. "Someone you didn't know twenty-four hours ago."

"Before you ask why, I'll tell you," he said, anticipating her next response. "I've got a hunch you're a good person to have on my side," he told her as she finished her dinner. "And if you ask why, I'll direct you back to the word *hunch*. Can't explain it any better than that."

"I sleep with a gun," she told him pointedly.

"I'm sure you do." And then he grinned. "Just so you know, so do I. In case you decide to have your way with me in the middle of the night—*if* you've decided to take me up on my offer."

It *would* make things simpler, she supposed. And there was the point he made about joining forces to discover where the girls were being kept so that they could choose the best girls. Two sets of eyes searching for the location where the girls were being housed was better than one; there was no denying that.

Okay, she'd play along until she could ascertain if Janie was being kept with the others, or if, for some reason, she was being housed somewhere else. In either case, Tiana needed to get her sister out. She planned to notify the local police about the location, hopefully as soon as she had her sister clear of the area.

"Okay, I'll take you up on your offer," she told him. "But at the first sign of you switching sides and turning on me, I will shoot you," she said. "Consider yourself warned."

Brennan shook his head. "You must be the real life of the party when you get going," he deadpanned.

"This isn't a party," she reminded him. "This is business, remember?"

"Never forgot for a second," he assured her, putting on his most serious face. "You want anything else?" he asked, nodding at the empty plate in front of her. Her serving had been as large as his and she'd done justice to it.

Anything else? Tiana tensed immediately. Had she just inadvertently left herself wide open? "What do you mean?"

"To eat," he specified. "Do you want anything else to eat? Like dessert?"

"Oh."

She felt just a wee bit foolish. *Just because you're paranoid doesn't mean they're not after you,* she reminded herself. It was far better to be cautious than to blindly walk into something.

"No, thanks," Tiana told him. "I'm stuffed." And she was. "You were right. The prime rib *is* good here." She looked around the dingy restaurant again. It was not a place that grew on you, she thought. "I guess they spend all their money on the food, not the décor."

This time the laugh escaping his lips was genuine. "You see any décor?" he asked.

"Actually, I see dust, not décor," she observed. "How do they manage to stay open?" she asked. When he looked at her quizzically, she elaborated. "Doesn't the health department periodically send inspectors to check the place out?"

"Palms get greased in all walks of life," he guessed. "But the guy in the kitchen takes great pride in his cooking—not so much in his housekeeping," he added. "Still, I don't think you'll ever catch anything eating here," Brennan assured her.

Taking out a hundred-dollar bill, he added a twenty to it as a tip and left both bills in the middle of the table. The chief had told him he needed to play up his part as a high roller because there was no telling when someone from the organization they were looking to bring down might be watching him.

"Let's go," he prompted, rising to his feet.

Tiana had taken note of the prices on the menu, intending to pay her own way so he didn't have an excuse to take his money out in trade later. What they'd had for dinner didn't come anywhere close to a hundred dollars.

"You always throw that kind of money around?" she asked him.

Brennan inclined his head. "Maybe I identify with the workingman—and -woman," he tossed in just in case "Venus" was the kind who took offense at accidental omissions.

"You really are a complicated man, aren't you?"

"Naw. What you see is what you get," he told her. The next moment, he placed his hand on the small of her back and guided her out.

Tiana *knew* it was her imagination, but she could almost *feel* the imprint of his hand against her back. Against her skin. It was almost as if all the layers of clothing had just burned away and there was nothing left between her and this man. Nothing left to protect her from this man's touch.

Get a grip, she ordered herself.

Once they were outside, the night air brought a chill with it that helped her focus and consequently caused her senses to wake up.

"Your car is still parked in the motel lot," she reminded him.

"No problem," he answered. "You can take me there in the morning."

"You don't want to pick it up now?" she asked, surprised. She would have thought that a man like him would have wanted the independence of his own car—unless he was going to take over hers. She hadn't thought of that until now.

He shook his head in answer to her question. "I don't know about you, but I'm pretty tired and I'd rather not drive under those conditions."

He was just full of surprises, she thought. "A careful criminal. Interesting."

"That's how you get to live long enough to become an *old* criminal," he pointed out, amused at her comment.

"You're not afraid that someone might steal it?" she prodded. "It's a pretty nice piece of work."

"There are ways of getting it back," he assured her. He had a sophisticated, top-of-the line GPS in the car, as well as a way to completely disable the car. Reaching her car, Brennan waited for her to unlock it. He got in on his side and buckled up. "Let me tell you where we're going," he said.

Most likely straight to hell in a toboggan, she said silently.

She braced herself for whatever it was that was waiting for her because she was willing to put up with anything to get Janie back.

She had to. Because Janie's safety and welfare were her responsibility, and always would be.

"What's up with you, Dad?" Andrew asked.

They had just had, by his standards, an incredibly quiet dinner, not to mention exceedingly small as far as company went. It had been just Rose, his father and him at the table, not by his design, but by Rose's.

Rose insisted that he get back into "the game" as she referred to his culinary efforts for the masses, otherwise known as his family, slowly. This, he had complained to no avail, was more restricting than having training wheels strapped onto a motorcycle. But Rose had told him that it was this, or she would be the one preparing dinner for his father. Everyone knew that Rose's efforts began and ended with picking up a telephone receiver and calling any one of a number of local restaurants that also delivered.

So he had given in and appeased his wife by making a tray of chicken tetrazzini for dinner. Afterward,

Rose, sensing her father-in-law's obvious somber mood, had withdrawn to allow him to have some privacy with his father and hopefully find out exactly what had brought this on.

"Nothing's up with me," Shamus protested in response to his question, but his mood continued to appear darker than a pending storm. He sat at the table, nursing the bottle of beer Rose had brought him instead of coffee.

Andrew studied his father. He'd been like this for a good few weeks. It wasn't like the old man. "I thought after I located your brother's family, you'd be doing handstands."

"Not a pretty sight," Shamus assured his oldest son. "But you did good, finding them," he allowed, nodding a head that still sported a full complement of thick silver hair.

"So why do you look as if you just realized you'd lost your best friend?" Andrew asked.

Shamus looked at him sharply. "'Why'?" he echoed. "You don't know 'why'?"

"Wouldn't be asking if I knew, Dad," Andrew said matter-of-factly, prepared to ride this storm out for as long as it took to get to the bottom of things.

Shamus set down his bottle of half-finished beer on the table and looked at him, really *looked* at him to the point that Andrew could almost feel his father's eyes boring into his face.

Then, in a low, harsh whisper, he told his firstborn, "Don't you ever, *ever* do that to me again, you hear? I won't stand for it."

"Do *what,* Dad? Stand for *what?*" Andrew pressed. So far, his father seemed to be going around in circles and he had no idea what the old man was driving at.

Shamus's eyes narrowed into slits and just for a moment, Andrew thought he saw them glint.

Tears?

"I lost one son," Shamus finally said in the same low, harsh tone. "I can't lose another. I can't go through that again, do you hear?"

Now it was starting to make sense to him. Whenever his father was really worried or overwhelmed with emotion, the only way he knew how to express it was through a display of anger. Softer words only came to him when he spoke to his grandchildren.

His father was referring to the night he'd gotten shot. "It's not exactly like I saw it coming, Dad," Andrew pointed out. As far as he was concerned, that homicidal maniac who'd almost killed him had just darted out of nowhere.

"Why not?" Shamus demanded angrily. "You're the one with eyes in the back of your head."

Andrew laughed and shook his head. "You're confusing me with Brian." He was aware of what the rank and file said about his younger brother, that as the chief of Ds, Brian was always one step ahead of everyone, always knew things before anyone else did. "He's the one with eyes in the back of his head. I'm the wise one."

"Wise one, huh," Shamus snorted. "Some wise one. If Fergus's boy hadn't been out there, pretending to be some hobo—"

"They call them homeless people now, Dad." Not that his father would remember that. He hadn't the other ten times Andrew had corrected him on the subject. The old man had a selective memory when it came to what he wanted to retain and what he didn't.

Shamus waved one sun-wrinkled, dismissive hand at the picky correction. It wasn't worth the effort to retain the information.

"Whatever. Point is if the good Lord hadn't had him there, you wouldn't be sitting here, correcting your betters, and I'd be standing in front of another tombstone, trying to explain to your mother how I could have let this happen."

Amusement highlighted Andrew's patrician features. "You do realize that you can't control everything, right, Dad?"

Shamus slanted an indignant glare his way that had more show than substance. "Says who?"

Andrew laughed. "Mom, for one, if she were still with us."

"Oh, she's with us, don't you ever doubt it," his father told him firmly. He never believed anything more in his life. "Right here—" the old man tapped his still somewhat muscular chest with his closed fist "—she's right here, with us."

Andrew merely nodded, knowing better than to get into a discussion with his father when he was in the sensitive mood he appeared to be in.

Glancing at his wristwatch, he saw that it was past ten. "It's getting kind of late, Dad. Why don't you and 'Mom' stay for the night?" he suggested. "We've got a lot of empty bedrooms just going begging, now that all five of the kids are out of the house."

"Not a bad idea," Shamus agreed, rising. "I am a wee bit tired—and I know when *not* to drive." Andrew began to get up, too, but his father waved him back into his chair. "It's not like I don't know where the bedrooms are," he said. "Your mother and I'll just pick one of them."

Rose, who chose that moment to reenter the dining room, raised an eyebrow as she looked at her husband.

"Your mother?" she mouthed.

"Long story," Andrew mouthed back.

"I look forward to it," Rose responded, then turned toward her father-in-law. "C'mon, Shamus, I'll get you some fresh sheets," she offered.

"I never argue with a lady," Shamus told her with an ingratiating smile.

Andrew snorted. "No, he saves that for me."

"How else are you going to stay on your toes?" Shamus asked. "The pots and pans aren't going to do it for you" were his parting words as the old man left the room.

Rose offered her husband an impish smile over her shoulder just before she accompanied her father-in-law out of the room.

Chapter 8

While it was not as opulent as the hotel where Roland was staying, Tiana had to admit that the Ambassador Hotel, where "Wayne" had brought her, was still light-years away in appearance from the motel that had turned out to be Wayne's final resting place.

She did her best to divorce herself from the notion that the motel might also have sheltered her sister, as well, before Janie vanished. For the most part, Tiana was trying very hard not to allow any negative thoughts about Janie's current state or her possible fate seep into her consciousness. If they got through, she had an uneasy feeling, the thoughts would wind up paralyzing her, and right now she needed all systems to be in top form if she was going to be of *any* helpful use to Janie.

And to be that, Tiana knew she had to survive her association with "Wayne" or whatever his real name actually was.

Unlike Roland's suite, where Wayne was staying was tasteful without being "in-your-face flashy." She supposed the proper term for the room might have been "understated"—just like the man himself.

"How much does staying in a place like this set you back?" she asked him as she looked around the two-room suite.

"It doesn't," Brennan said. "That's the whole point."

She turned to look at him, a dubious expression on her face.

Yeah, right.

"They're just letting you stay here out of the kindness of their hearts," she concluded, mocking the very suggestion. Exactly how stupid did he think she was?

"No, of course there's a charge. But you didn't ask that. You asked if it set me back, and it doesn't. The amount is something that I'm able to pay without thinking about and it has no effect on what I can afford and what I can't afford," he told her.

As he spoke, Brennan made his way easily around the room, seeming to aimlessly glance about. What he was actually doing was checking certain items in the suite to see if they'd been moved even the tiniest bit. He'd carefully placed those items at angles that were not obvious but if disturbed would have been immediately noticeable to him.

Everything was where it was supposed to be. There were no bugs planted. Nothing had been removed, either. That meant he wasn't on anyone's radar yet. The operative word being *yet.* He was very aware of the fact that he was operating on borrowed time.

"If something 'sets you back,' that means you have to budget to make sure the rest of your ends meet. I gave up that sort of painful existence when I made up my mind to go into 'the life.'"

"The life," she repeated. Wayne had to be talking about sex trafficking. Was he trying to clean it up for her benefit? Or his own? "Is that how you refer to it?"

His response was accompanied with a grin. "Sounds a lot better than flesh peddling and sex trafficking, doesn't it?"

It didn't matter what he called it, it still was what it was, she thought fiercely. By *any* name, kidnapping young girls and forcing them or coaxing them into a life of sexual servitude was not only wrong, it was downright *evil.*

"A rose by any other name still has thorns," she told him.

He inclined his head as if giving her version its due. "Nice twist—and also true. But I'm not interested in wearing a hair shirt and meditating on sin—unless, of course, that sin turns out to be entertaining," he quipped, looking pointedly at her.

His answer was less than comforting. Maybe, just maybe, she couldn't help thinking, she'd gotten in over her head and she was going to have to stay alert the whole time she was here.

Leaving briefly crossed her mind, but she had to admit that this man was still her best bet to work her way into the organization and find out where her sister was being kept.

Much as Tiana hated to admit it, right now she needed this man.

"I suppose it's all in the way you view the word *entertainment*," she replied.

He seemed to decrease the space between them without actually taking a step. It was his manner that did it. He could make all this sound very personal with just a look. *Too* personal, actually.

"How do you view it?" he asked her in a low voice that, though she hated to admit it to herself, seemed to undulate along her skin.

She knew she had to say something, but it really didn't need to make that much sense. "That, lucky for you, is none of your concern."

This time he did cut the space between them and stood right over her. "Try me."

He was standing way too close, invading her space and she didn't like that she could feel the heat rising from his body, reaching out to her. She liked even less that it was disarming her. How could she *possibly* be attracted to a man like this?

And, on the flip side, Tiana knew she couldn't possibly have any allure for him—other than the fact that if he felt he couldn't have something, like a spoiled child, that was the one thing he wanted.

Right now *she* was that one thing.

Tiana raised her chin. "I'll pass."

"Not interested?" Brennan asked, his tone somewhat amused. Ordinarily, the women he saw socially, when he had the opportunity to be himself, were around her age as well as her general description—although he had to admit he'd never gone out with a redhead.

He told himself to get his mind back on business.

"I said I'll pass," she pointed out. "Nothing was said about being 'interested' one way or another. Now, I think we're both tired and we need to get some sleep. I'm willing to take the couch." She nodded toward the piece of furniture that, all things considered, looked to be comfortable.

He was *not* going to go roundabout with her. There was a very practical reason for his decision. One he was not about to tell her.

"You'll take the bed and that's the end of it. I'm not chivalrous very often, so make the most of it." He glanced toward the bathroom. "Since there's only one shower, we'll work out a schedule as to 'who gets ready when' in the morning."

"I can hardly wait," she deadpanned.

The smile on his face went straight to her nerve center, systematically destroying anything and everything it came in contact with.

And that was on a glass of water, Tiana realized. She was damn grateful she hadn't had anything strong to drink, because God only knew what might happen in the next few hours if her guard was down and her inhibitions had gone off on a holiday.

"Me, too," he concurred, commenting on her last crack.

She had to stop letting him affect her like that, she

silently lectured. "I'll get ready for bed first," she told him. "Unless you have any objections."

He shook his head, looking more endearingly charming than any man—especially given his profession—had a right to be. "Not a one."

She slipped her weapon out of her purse and tucked it into her waistband. It was done purely as a warning. "By the way, in case you're wondering, I'm taking my gun with me."

"Wouldn't have it any other way," he agreed with a straight face. "Careful not to get it waterlogged."

He was making fun of her, she thought. The next moment, she upbraided herself for reacting in any fashion. It didn't matter what he said. He could say whatever he wanted to as long as in the end he was instrumental in leading her to Janie. At that point, everything else would be balanced out.

Tiana was never one to take a long time getting ready for bed. There was no long, drawn-out ritual she undertook to make certain that wrinkles remained a word used on the side of enhancement bottles and didn't set up residence on her skin.

Tonight she got ready probably faster than she ever had before. Eight minutes after she went into the bathroom, she came out again and was about to announce, "It's all yours," when she stopped dead in her tracks, stunned.

Wayne's back was to her and she had emerged from the bathroom without making a sound. Years of moving around, trying not to wake her father who'd fallen asleep at the table after emptying a bottle of whiskey, had taught her how to be incredibly quiet. Consequently, the man called Wayne hadn't heard her when she came out.

She couldn't believe what it appeared he was doing. Oh, she knew exactly what it looked like, knew what he was most likely doing, but she heard herself asking, anyway, on the outside chance that maybe she was wrong. Maybe he could actually come up with a plausible explanation for going through her purse.

Although she highly doubted it.

"What are you doing?" she asked in a low, steely voice, pointing her gun at him.

The sound of her voice—he'd thought she was still in the bathroom—startled him, but he'd gotten years of practice at not reacting and he didn't this time. Instead, he smoothly answered, "Looking for a cell phone charger."

Well, that was certainly an imaginative response. "In my purse?" she challenged.

He nonchalantly closed her purse and put it on the coffee table in front of him. "Seemed like a logical place to start. I misplaced mine," he explained with a shrug.

"That's the best you've got?" she asked him incredulously.

"The truth is never fancy."

He was good, oh, he was good, she thought. Not with the answers he came up with, but he did deliver them in an unflappable manner. However, unflappable or not, she wasn't buying it.

She kept her weapon trained on him.

"The truth is also not anywhere close to what's coming out of your mouth. Now, *why* are you riffling through my purse?" she demanded. She *knew* she should have taken it in with her, but she thought he'd use the time to look through her suitcase rather than her purse since there were more compartments for her to hide something—which was exactly why she didn't keep anything incriminating in there.

If being caught in the act made him uncomfortable, the man staring down the business end of her weapon didn't show it in the slightest. "I wanted to see if you were on the level."

The man was very cool under fire, she had to give him that. "My word's not good enough, I take it."

"Not until I know you better."

"What about all this I-got-your-back stuff?" she challenged.

"That's what it is for now, 'stuff.' When and if I get to know you better, then our alliance might actually fall into the I've-got-your-back category." He paused, knowing he was taking a chance and really pushing his luck, but his gut told him it would turn out all right. "Who's the girl in your wallet?" he asked. "Is she the reason you're looking for strawberry blondes?"

Tiana froze. The photo he was referring to was the one she'd been showing to people as she searched for Janie. There was another photograph in her wallet, as well. It was of the two of them, taken right after her sister's graduation from high school. Someone she'd shown it to back in San Francisco had commented that he could see a strong family resemblance in that photograph.

Back then, it had been just her and Janie. Wayne hadn't entered the picture yet.

She should have sheltered her sister more. But she'd done just the opposite, she'd loosened the strict, confining rules her father had imposed on Janie, letting her sister experience freedom of choice. She'd done it because she wanted Janie to feel independent, to make her own decisions.

Maybe if she had closed ranks, protected Janie a little better, all of this, including facing down a cocky flesh peddler, would never have had to happen.

Tiana bit her lip, trying to think. What did she do with Wayne now that he was onto her? She'd just started to trust him a little, too.

And that had been a big mistake, she realized.

The next minute, she raised her gun higher, as if to take direct aim at his chest.

"I'm really sorry you had to see that," she said. "If you'd just left things alone…"

"Who is she?" Brennan asked again.

Oh, what the hell did it matter if he knew? Her cover, at least with him, was blown. Which meant he had to be eliminated as a threat. But how? She couldn't just shoot him. She needed to have him locked up somewhere where he couldn't get in her way or expose her.

"She's my sister," Tiana told him.

"And you're looking for her." It wasn't a guess, it was a statement.

A sarcastic smile curved her mouth. "Give the man a prize."

"Well, if you feel that way about it," he quipped, turning on his charm, "you could start by lowering your gun."

Instead, she cocked the hammer. "Think again," she suggested.

His eyes never left her face. "You don't want to shoot me."

Her laugh was harsh and without any humor at all. "I repeat, think again."

"If you discharge that weapon, the sound will bring security running. You won't be able to get away."

Just how naive did he think she was? "Ever hear of using a pillow as a silencer?"

He continued looking into her eyes. "You're not a killer."

"Well, there you're wrong," she told him, fishing out her cell phone. "Everyone's a killer given the right set of circumstances."

"These are not those circumstances," he told her.

Unbelievable, she thought. The man had to have better nerves than she did. "You're awfully cocky for a man with a gun pointed at him."

"Remember what I said about needing to look into a person's eyes when I talk to her?" he asked her. He didn't wait for her to acknowledge the conversation. "Yours tell me you're not a killer."

Lucky guess, she thought as she opened her phone. "Mine aren't saying anything to you. But for the record, I'm not going to kill you. But I *am* going to turn you over to the local police and let them deal with you." To her surprise and no small annoyance, the man facing the business end of her weapon started to laugh. "What's so funny?" she demanded.

He sobered slightly. "You'll find out," he promised. "The chief of detectives is a man named Brian Cavanaugh. You might ask to be connected directly to him," he suggested. "It'll save time."

She was in no hurry to do anything he might have suggested, "Why? Is he in your back pocket?" Tiana accused. She couldn't see any other reason why Wayne would tell her the name of someone in the police department to contact unless he had that man on his personal payroll.

The chief of detectives, no less—this man certainly didn't believe in wasting time dealing with underlings.

"I promise you, Brian Cavanaugh is in *nobody's* pocket, back or front," Brennan told her.

She was not about to be lulled into complacency, or walk into a trap for that matter. "If you don't mind, I'll do it my way."

He spread his hands innocently, then raised them again when she looked as if she was taking aim at his chest a second time. "Don't mind at all."

Wayne was being way too cooperative, Tiana couldn't help thinking. Did that mean he intended to get the jump on her, overpower her at some point and then turn the tables by eliminating her?

She no longer knew *what* to think.

Brennan decided to try one last time to talk her down. "Look, you seem to be a decent enough person

and I don't want you to embarrass yourself by bringing me in—"

She was immediately suspicious—even more than
she already was. "And just how would I embarrass
myself doing that, 'Wayne'?" she asked.

"Well, to start with," he began, "my name isn't
Bruce Wayne."

As if *that* hadn't been hopelessly transparent. "Big
surprise," she taunted.

He disregarded her tone and continued talking. "My
name's Brennan and I'm working undercover to bring
the ring down. The same ring you think has your sister," he elaborated.

This man was really quick on his feet, she thought
grudgingly. He wasn't even breaking a sweat. She had
a feeling, though, that if he'd been a character in a
fairy tale, his nose would already be a mile long. "Of
course you are."

Brennan knew it was futile, but he told her, "It's
the truth."

Now, there was a joke. "I don't think you'd know
the truth if it sat up and bit you," she responded with
contempt.

Tiana decided not to bother calling the station but
just bring him in. She cuffed him with handcuffs she'd
had hidden in the lining of her purse. To avoid attract-
ing undue attention, she cuffed his hands in front of
him and draped a jacket over the cuffs.

"Now we're going to walk out of this hotel nice and
slow and then I'm going to drive us to the police station, where they can throw you into a cell and you can

rot for all I care." The smile on her lips was forced. "Do I make myself clear?"

He supposed there was no other way to go about this. He wasn't planning on overpowering her—although the thought had its tempting merits. But guns were not exactly a stable factor in this kind of a mix. They'd been known to discharge when two people wrestled for possession, and he didn't want to take that chance. Besides, being handcuffed did put him at a slight disadvantage. Going along with her on this seemed like the best way that neither one of them would get hurt. And now he knew what she was doing there—and that she had to be exceptionally resourceful to have put together all the pieces and made it to this plateau in such a short amount of time.

"Sounds like a plan to me," he agreed.

Red flags were going off all over the place. Something was off. "I can't figure out if you're being very cooperative or very stupid."

"I'd go along with both if I were you. That way you hedge your bets and win either way. Ready to go any time you are," he told her cheerfully.

He was being way too cheerful. Something was wrong, but she didn't have the time to try to figure out what. Let the Aurora police department sort it out once she handed him over. Because then he officially became *their* problem.

"Better stay really close to me in the lobby," he advised. "You don't want me to make a break for it, do you?"

In response, she took hold of his upper arm, hold-

ing on to it as tightly as she could. He was rather surprised at the amount of strength she had. The woman
had a lot of impressive things going for her.

"I'm glad you think this is such a joke," she bit off.

"No joke," he corrected. "Just being helpful."

She ushered him into the elevator, keeping her
weapon out of sight but nonetheless ready. "This
doesn't feel right," she said aloud.

"What?"

"This," she bit off. "You. Being so cooperative. It
just doesn't feel right." She felt herself growing edgier.
She had no idea what to be braced for.

"Maybe I've seen the error of my ways," he said as
they reached the ground floor.

"And maybe the moon is made of green cheese,"
she retorted, ushering him through the lobby and out
through the entrance.

"Maybe," he agreed.

"Stop talking," she ordered, hustling him over toward her vehicle.

"Yes, ma'am," he replied obediently. But as she
pushed him into the passenger seat, then quickly hurried to the other side and got in behind the steering
wheel, he broke his so-called silence by telling her,
"You'll want to take Jamboree Boulevard to Harvard.
Can't miss the building. It's right smack in the middle
between Jamboree and Main."

This was getting to be very weird. She knew where
the local police station was, having looked it up as a
point of reference when she came to Aurora so she

knew his directions were accurate. But that still didn't answer her question.

Why was he giving her directions? *Accurate* directions? Did he have some kind of backup plan in case he was captured?

Was she walking into some sort of trap?

No one had followed them from Roland's hotel; she'd paid strict attention to that.

Just what was this man's game?

By the time she reached the police station, a short distance away, her nerves were all but peeled down to the core.

Chapter 9

"Okay, let's go," Tiana said, motioning her prisoner out of the vehicle once she had opened the passenger-side door.

Rather than complying, the man she knew as "Wayne" remained where he was. There was no way she could physically haul him out of there if he didn't want to go.

She might have the gun in her hand, but she couldn't very well just shoot the man no matter how tempting or appealing the notion might be at the moment.

Brennan watched her, amusement highlighting his ruggedly handsome face. He could see her getting progressively angrier at him.

"Are you sure you want to do this?" he asked the pseudomadam.

It was hard to hold on to a temper that was becoming so frayed, especially when she was as tired as she was. Once she handed this man over to the police, she intended to go back to his room—no point in letting a perfectly good paid-for room go to waste, she reasoned—and get a good night's sleep.

"So you've changed your mind about cooperating, have you?" She grabbed hold of his arm, indicating that she was ready to drag him out if need be—she just hoped he wouldn't call her bluff, because she could feel her strength waning even as she was standing here.

"No, I'm still cooperating," he told her cheerfully. "I'm just pointing out that maybe this might not be the best course of action for you to take."

He had to say that, she reasoned—but how could he possibly think she might even remotely agree with what he was suggesting?

"Bringing a sex trafficker to the local police station, how can I go wrong doing that?" she asked.

Brennan only grinned wider. "I guess you'll just have to find out."

Tiana narrowed her eyes and she pointed her handgun at him. Enough was enough. "Get out of the car," she ordered.

"You're the boss," he said in an utterly innocent tone.

Wayne's very demeanor should have warned her that what he was saying might actually be on the level, but then, she had a feeling this man could *and* would brazen it out to the very end.

She was also convinced that this person was a very

accomplished, smooth liar, skillful at making just about anything sound like the truth.

"Just move," she told him in a voice that barely suppressed her anger.

She kept her weapon hidden against his back as she directed him toward the modern looking building. They crossed the short distance from where she had parked her car in the lot to the steps of the police station. Her prisoner offered no resistance.

The second she walked through the automatic doors behind her handcuffed prisoner, all sorts of alarms went off, sounding like the church bells in Westminster Abbey at Christmas.

Within a heartbeat, Tiana found herself surrounded by half a dozen police officers.

The blue-clad officers flooded into the main lobby, their weapons drawn and aimed directly at them.

More specifically, since Brennan had entered ahead of her and the alarms had gone off when she followed behind him, the officers' weapons were aimed at her.

Brennan heard her stifling a sharp gasp. Looking at his would-be jailer over his shoulder, he said, "Now, this is just a wild guess on my part—and I might be wrong—but those alarms going off like that might have something to do with the gun in your possession."

"Put the weapon down!" ordered the tall officer who was at the center of the armed guard facing them.

She glared at "Wayne" as she complied with the order, following through with exaggerated motions so that there was no mistake made as to what she was doing.

Once she'd placed her handgun on the floor and risen, her hands automatically raised in surrender, she told the officers, "My name is Tiana Drummond. I'm with the San Francisco CSI unit." She went on to give her badge number, taking care to enunciate each number. She knew someone would be verifying her identity the second she gave the last number. "I don't know this man's real name, but he's involved with a sex trafficking ring that's kidnapping underage girls."

To her relief, she saw the officer who'd issued the order lower his weapon, then holstered it. The others all followed suit.

They believed her, Tiana thought with a grateful sigh.

The slender blond officer at the extreme left came forward, shaking her head. When she spoke, it wasn't Tiana she addressed but the man Tiana had brought in.

"Jeez, Brennan," the blonde cried, "why didn't you tell her you were an undercover cop?"

Brennan grinned at Valri, his youngest sister and the family's newest law enforcement officer. Valri had graduated from the academy just in time to have her options doubled, allowing her to choose between the police department at Shady Canyon and the one here, in Aurora. Out of loyalty to him, she'd decided to move to Aurora.

Brennan presented his handcuffed wrists to his "captor," waiting for her to do the honors. He heard a rather exasperated sigh escape her a second before he felt her opening up his handcuffs.

Freed, he rubbed his wrists. "Well, I kind of tried,"

he told Valri, "but she kept wanting her gun to do the talking for her, and you know me, I don't like arguing with a lady."

It was Valri's turn to be amused. She laughed at the very suggestion of what he'd tried to pass off as the truth. "Since when? All you ever do is argue. You *live* for it."

"That's at home," Brennan pointed out. "I'm nicer outside."

Tiana had heard more than enough. Getting in between the two siblings, she cried, "Wait a minute. You were actually serious?" she demanded, her tone nothing short of accusing as she looked at the man she had just arrested and brought in. "You really *are* a cop?"

Summoned by the receptionist the moment the duo had entered the building, Brian Cavanaugh walked into the lobby in time to hear the last exchange.

"Yes, he really is a cop."

Turning her head in the direction the deep voice was coming from, Tiana noticed a tall, almost larger-than-life distinguished-looking man coming toward her.

The man introduced himself, extending his hand. "I'm chief of detectives Brian Cavanaugh and the man you just brought in is working undercover for my department. Meet Detective First Class Brennan Cavanaugh. And you are?" he asked politely, giving her a chance to formerly introduce herself to him even though he had already heard her name, thanks to the two-way radio in his possession. It was tuned in to the receptionist's area.

"Stunned and embarrassed," Tiana replied, staring at Brennan. Her eyes narrowed as she glared at him—right now, for her own satisfaction, she had to blame *someone* for this mistake. And he was it. "Why didn't you *tell* me?"

"I did. I tried," he corrected. "You wouldn't listen." He glanced at his newly discovered uncle. As far as he knew, he hadn't heard her name when she'd stated it. "Chief, this is—"

The least she could do was give her own name, Tiana thought grudgingly, especially since she'd apparently messed up everything else.

"CSI Tiana Drummond, sir," she said, shaking the hand the chief had offered.

"Tiana, huh?" Brennan rolled her name over on his tongue. "I think I like Venus better."

Brian looked from his nephew to the woman who had brought him in. Obviously there were a few more things that needed clearing up. "Venus?"

"It's part of my cover," Tiana quickly explained. "Or at least the name he—" she nodded at Brennan "—decided he liked better."

Brian shook his head. "Forgive me, Detective, but I don't—"

She flashed an understanding smile at him. She could see how it would be confusing to someone who hadn't been there to begin with. "It's a long story, sir."

Brian took the disclaimer at face value. "Why don't we go to my office and you can tell it?" he suggested to the young woman. He looked around at the semi-circle of police officers who were still in the lobby.

"You can stand down now and go back to what you were doing," he told them.

As the officers began to disperse, Brian called after them, "By the way, good job, Officers," he told them with a smile of approval. Then, turning to his nephew and the young woman who had brought him in, he said, "Shall we go?"

"By all means, sir," Tiana answered, more than willing to leave the scene of her embarrassing error.

As she followed the tall, imposing man to the rear of the lobby where the elevators were, she couldn't help wondering if she was going to ultimately get a formal dressing-down. After all, she had in effect "arrested" the chief of detectives' nephew.

"Your superiors don't know you're down here, do they?" the man asked her as they waited for an elevator to arrive.

It sounded like a rhetorical question, one that if he posed, he probably already had the answer to. But to assume he did and not answer would be rude, she figured, so Tiana said, "No, sir, they don't. I took a leave of absence."

"Why didn't you enlist their help?" he asked.

That might have been the logical course of action to someone observing from the outside. But she had her reasons.

"Because this is personal, sir," she told him. They got into the elevator, its only occupants, and the doors closed again. "I didn't want everyone I work with to have any reason to look down on my sister. This is already hard enough on her as it is."

"You know better, Detective," Brian pointed out.

"No, sir," she contradicted him, much to Brennan's surprise. "I know people, I know life, and it's only natural to assume the worst about a person. My sister was lied to by a man she thought loved her. A man who used that 'love' to reel her in—in effect kidnap her—and turn her over to his boss, another low-level lowlife. As far as I know, she and whatever other girls had been either lured or abducted are going to ultimately be sent off to any one of a number of foreign countries—or enslaved in this country and shipped off to some other, unknown state. Either way, she'll be made to disappear along with the others. To a lot of people, Janie is just another teenage prostitute, another potential statistic. I won't have her judged."

"You don't know that for sure," he pointed out. "Sometimes you just have to take a chance and let others help you."

They reached his floor and got out, with Brian half a step ahead, leading the way.

She didn't want to argue about whether or not she should have told her superiors about this. Instead, she pointed out a logical assumption and its ensuing implication.

"The case is in your jurisdiction now. The traffickers are here, somewhere in the Aurora vicinity. That makes this your case, sir."

"Yes, it does," he agreed. He walked into his office and indicated the chairs before his desk. He sat down behind it and waited for the duo to take their seats. He kept his eyes on the young woman, but his thoughts were impossible to gauge.

Tiana found that frustrating. She was hardly aware of sitting down, her attention riveted on the chief. "Does that mean that you'll be working it?" she asked, needing him to spell it out for her.

"We already are," Brennan said. He'd kept quiet up until now, but this he was qualified to talk about, especially since he was the one on the inside. "What part of 'undercover' don't you understand?" he asked, referring to the words he'd used to tell her that he was part of a covert operation.

She shrugged, feeling both frustrated and flustered at the same time. "It's not so much a matter of not understanding as it is not believing," she admitted. "I believe you now."

"We'll take it from here," Brian assured her kindly. "If you have a picture of your sister, I can circulate it around, have my people be alerted to her status. All due precautions will be taken to keep her safe," he promised her. "You have my word."

Tiana took out her wallet and handed over the picture that had caused her to arrest Brennan in the first place.

Brian looked at the photograph for a long moment. "She's a very pretty girl," he commented. "We'll find her," he promised again. Taking a breath—knowing how he would have felt if it had been his daughter, Janelle, who had been abducted—he banked down a wave of empathy. "Where can you be reached?"

"I'll be with him," Tiana responded, nodding toward Brennan, her eyes still on the chief.

Brian's expression was solemn. "I can't sanction you for this operation in your official capacity, Tiana. I have no jurisdiction over you and you in turn have none here."

She had expected nothing less. Her mouth curved slightly as she looked at the chief. "Then as far as you know, I'm not here."

They were definitely getting into a sticky gray area. "But you are."

She decided to be completely honest with him and make her plea.

"Chief Cavanaugh, Janie is the only family I have. I *can't* just go back to San Francisco and sit on my hands, waiting for sanitized updates from either your office or your nephew. Please," she added in an emotion-filled, heartfelt plea.

It was a situation that had already come up before and would, Brian knew, come up again. The ranks were filled with family members. In this young woman's place, he would have felt exactly the same way. Hell, in *his* place he would have felt exactly the same and he had more relatives than any other random handful of people put together.

Brian looked at her and said in a deliberate, measured cadence, "I don't have the authority to escort you back to San Francisco. I can only tell you to go home. Which I just did." He half rose in his seat, signaling the meeting was over. "Now, if you'll both excuse me, I unfortunately have to face the media at a news conference. It seems that word of these traffickers and their abductions has spread and I have to assure the good people of Aurora through those news vultures circling outside that everything is being done to bring the missing girls back home and to bring to justice the people who abducted them."

Brian looked at the young man who had so recently come to his attention and who had literally saved his older brother's life. "Keep me apprised as best you can, and the second you have either a name or the location where the girls are being kept, call for backup. Immediately," he stressed.

"Count on it," Brennan promised.

"A name?" Tiana questioned as they left the chief's office. This time, Brennan directed her toward the freight elevator, which let out in a more secluded part of the building.

They made their way down to the ground floor.

"The name of the head of this whole ring. The chief is of the same opinion that we are, that there's someone behind the scenes pulling all the strings. Roland is *not* the main man, even though he struts around like he is. He's taking his orders from someone, and the second I can find out who that person is, we can have the whole place crawling with police."

He'd forgotten one salient point she'd made. "But not before we find where the girls are being held." It was more of a plea than a comment.

Despite his easygoing disposition, Brennan was a realist. Things didn't always turn out the way people wanted them to.

"Hopefully," he said, "we can do both."

On the ground floor, she stopped walking and turned to face him. "You can't call in backup until we have the location," she insisted. "The girls are expendable to these people. They'll kill them rather than be caught with them."

Brennan looked impressed. "You're not as naive as I thought you were," he told her. "And I mean 'naive' in the best possible way," he added with a smile in case he'd accidentally insulted her.

She pushed open the glass door and hurried down the stairs to the parking lot. "I'm not naive at all," Tiana told him. Reaching her vehicle, she got in and waited for him to do the same. As he was buckling up, she started the car. "Except when it comes to a one-on-one relationship," she added in a lower voice.

The admission caught his attention. "Love turn sour on you, Venus?" he asked, curious.

"Love hasn't had an opportunity to turn anything at all on me," she responded. Life with her father had caused her to think not twice, but three times before even *considering* entering a relationship. And so far, she hadn't. "I've been too busy."

"What do you do for fun?" he asked.

She drove off the lot, heading back to his hotel. "Solve crimes."

"Besides that."

"I sleep." She held up the hand closest to him as if to warn him off. "And before you ask, no, I don't sleep much. I don't need to." Or at least, she had talked herself into this mind-set. "My batteries recharge themselves with amazing speed."

"You are one hell of an amazing woman, Venus," Brennan told her.

She could almost believe him. *Almost,* she silently stressed. In her experience she'd come to learn that men rarely spoke the truth.

Even men like him.

First and foremost, they were out for themselves. They were concerned with their comfort, their terms, their gain. Women and their needs or requirements came in a distant second—if they came in at all.

She changed the subject. "Are you really related to the chief?" she asked him.

"So it seems. He's my father's cousin. This is all very recent," he admitted. "There was this whole division of the family that I never knew anything about until about a month ago."

"You work here and you didn't know you were related?" Tiana asked, surprised.

"To understand, you'd have to know the full story."

"Okay, I'm listening," she said. He now knew a lot about her. In her opinion, it was his turn to come clean about things.

"I wasn't over here. I started out in Shady Canyon. I worked undercover for the DEA at the time," he interjected. "But I transferred over from the neighboring town when I was suspended for saving the former chief of police's life. Andrew Cavanaugh," he said, telling her the man's name. "And yes, turns out I'm related to him, as well."

This was getting pretty complicated and she was getting rather punchy at this point. She either needed a scorecard or some sleep in order to keep what he was telling her straight.

Tiana opted for sleep and held up her hand, signaling she wanted him to pause.

"Why don't you give me the full rundown once my mind kicks in tomorrow morning?" she suggested. The way she felt right now, she would have trouble following the story line within a nursery rhyme.

He grinned at her. "Deal. You're calling the shots here," was what he told her, but even in her less than sharp condition, she knew he was just humoring her. He was the one in charge and they both knew that.

However, she appreciated the lip service he'd just given. At this stage of the game, she would take whatever she could get.

"You sure you don't want to sit this out?" he asked her, his tone almost kind. "I promise that I'll keep you up to date on what's going on."

Did he think she was some empty-headed, frail little thing who could just be patted on the head and sent home to wait for the phone to ring? Boy, did he have the wrong person!

"No offense, Cavanaugh, but I can keep myself up to date by being right there."

"Look, Venus, you're too close to this whole thing."

"Don't you understand?" she asked, cutting him off, suddenly getting a second wind, however fleeting it might prove to be. "*Close* is the only way to solve this. This isn't something to be handled from a distance by remote control. And maybe having someone invested in the outcome, *really* invested, will provide that extra push that's needed to bring these scum down."

"Following that line of thinking, we'd have to say yes to all the fathers, all the parents of those missing girls if they wanted to take part in this operation and then we'd have something akin to the scene where the villagers storm the castle, carrying pitchforks and torches and yelling for someone's blood to be spilled."

"It's not the same thing," she insisted angrily. "I don't own a pitchfork and I don't have a torch. What I *do* have is law enforcement training. *That's* the difference. Now, if you have a problem with that, okay, I can't force you to take me with you."

She aroused his suspicions immediately. "That's too reasonable," he said.

"No," she pointed out, "it's what you want to hear." She shrugged as if she didn't care which path she took, as long as it got her to where she wanted to go. "I'll just do this on my own, that's all."

"That's what I *don't* want to hear," he said with a sigh, resigned. "I'd rather have you next to me, where I can keep my eye on you, than operating somewhere out there with me looking over my shoulder all the time, wondering exactly where you are and if you've gotten yourself into trouble. If nothing else, this way will be safer. For *both* of us," he emphasized.

The grin was self-satisfied and triumphant. "Good choice."

"I don't know about good," he told her as if he'd considered the matter from all sides, "but right now it's the only option open to me—other than tying you up and leaving you in a closet. With my luck, you probably know how to get out of every knot I learned how to make as a Boy Scout."

She didn't answer him. But her smile said it all. It told him that he'd made a pretty damn good guess.

Chapter 10

Having made her point, Tiana hardly remembered getting out of the elevator or walking down the hotel hallway to Brennan's room. Almost out of the blue, she'd been hit by an overwhelming wave of exhaustion.

Closing the door behind them, Brennan glanced in her direction—and then paused to look at her more closely. "No offense," he told her, "but you really look like you're wiped out."

He was right, but she absolutely hated appearing anything but up at the top of her game, ready to go on for hours. Her sense of competition wouldn't allow her to admit he was right in his assessment.

"Give me a second and I'll be ready to go another five rounds or more," she promised, sinking down onto the sofa.

"Then you'll have to find someone else to go those rounds with, because I'm pretty wiped out myself," Brennan told her.

As he spoke, he moved slowly through the area, checking everything in the double-room suite to make certain that no one had been there.

Satisfied that nothing had been touched and no one had left any bugs or microdigital cameras for the purpose of covertly recording their movements and conversation, he turned around to see that she hadn't moved an inch off the sofa.

"The agreement was that you take the bed and I take the sofa, and that hasn't changed," he pointed out, crossing back to her. "I'm a man of my word—and you are a woman fast asleep," he realized with a resigned sigh now that he was closer to her.

Brennan debated picking her up—she didn't look as if she weighed more than a hundred, a hundred ten pounds—and putting her in bed. But with his luck, she'd wake up just as he set her down and she'd probably shoot him with some peashooter she had hidden away.

It was easier on both of them to just leave her where she was, he decided. Although, as he reassessed the situation, she was probably going to wake up with one hell of a stiff neck if she stayed in the exact same position she was in until morning.

To avoid that, he'd have to lay her down without waking her up, a tricky proposition at best.

"You sure don't make it easy for a guy, do you?" he muttered to himself.

If he had an iota of sense in his head, Brennan thought, he'd leave her like this, stiff neck be damned. But he couldn't do that. She just looked so damn vulnerable right now, he found himself feeling for her. He really had no choice in the matter.

The truth was, she stirred his sense of compassion and he felt sorry for her—although if he even *hinted* at that, he had a feeling she'd take his head off without so much as blinking an eye.

The vulnerability he saw went beyond just her appearance. She'd said that her sister was her only family, and he couldn't begin to imagine what that had to feel like. He'd *always* been aware of family from his very first memory somewhere around the age of about three. Family had always been the basic foundation of his life, a given he'd never even thought to question.

Even when he was on these lengthy assignments that took him away from everyone, in the back of his mind was the reassuring thought that they were there, his family, ready to step in with a word, a gesture—or actual backup if he was in a jam professionally and needed them to come in, guns drawn.

They had his back and he had theirs. That was just the way things were.

This woman sleeping in front of him didn't have that, and yet she was here, toughing it out, determined to go against all odds, straight into the belly of the beast to find and rescue her sister.

You had to admire a woman like that. Now if only she weren't so attractive. Her looks, her whole in-your-face personality, distracted him on many levels.

Having lowered Tiana onto the sofa so that her head rested against the cushioned arm, Brennan took a second to study her further. Asleep, all her hard edges, all her bravado, faded into the background, leaving the softer woman beneath exposed for viewing.

She looked even prettier this way, he realized.

Great, in danger up to your eyeballs and you're standing here like some wet-behind-the-ears rookie, rating her looks and having thoughts no way in hell you should be having.

Brennan reminded himself that this was not some stilted reality program. This was life, with a capital *L*. Real and hard and just possibly hiding death behind every corner. He had to remember that.

Once they got the bad guys, he could rate her looks and her manner. Right now he had enough to do keeping them both alive.

With a weary sigh, Brennan double-checked the locks on the door one last time. Deciding to take a very old-fashioned precaution—sometimes the old methods were the best ones—he dragged a chair over to the door. He then angled it beneath the doorknob so that it acted as barrier for anyone trying to break in by picking the lock or accessing entrance by somehow duplicating the key card he'd been issued.

Having the chair wedged in like that would allow it to make just enough noise if it was moved to wake him up. If he trained himself to sleep any lighter, a falling eyelash would wake him, he thought sarcastically.

"Okay, evening ritual completed," he murmured under his breath. "And the princess is still asleep," he noted, glancing in her direction. Nodding, he lowered himself into the chair that faced the door, his weapon drawn and ready, resting against his knees. "See you in the morning, Venus," he whispered to the woman on the sofa as he closed his eyes.

Tiana didn't wake up so much as she jackknifed up.

One moment she was on the sofa, her eyes still closed as she languidly stretched her body the way she did each morning as she tried to rouse herself into a wakeful state; the next she'd opened her eyes. Instead of being somewhere familiar—or at the very least, somewhere alone—she found herself on a sofa being studied by the man who had been part of her humiliating experience last night.

Her body fairly snapped into an upright position as if it had been preset on some sort of a spring mechanism that went off at the slightest touch.

"What are you doing?" she demanded, her heart launching into a hard, arrhythmic beat in response to the way he was looking at her.

"Right now I'm just waiting for you to wake up," he told her mildly.

"Right now," she repeated, trying to make some sort of sense out of what he was saying. "And before?"

It was obvious by the expression on his face that Brennan wasn't sure what she was referring to. "Before when?"

"Before 'right now,'" she emphasized, not knowing how to make it any clearer than that. Was he just trying to confuse her? Because if he was, he had damn well succeeded.

Tiana tried to remember how she had gotten in his hotel room and just how she'd wound up on the sofa. Right now all her thoughts seemed to be jumbled and there was this killer headache absorbing all parts of her.

After a moment, Brennan began to answer her. "Well, got dressed, showered, woke up—"

"Wait," she ordered, staring at him. "What? You got dressed, then showered?" she questioned incredulously.

Tiana looked at him warily. Was he crazy? Or was he just trying to make her feel that way?

"Of course not," he told her with a laugh. "I showered, then got dressed."

"But you just said—"

"You said you wanted me to recount what I'd done before now," he reminded her, cutting in. "I didn't know how far back you wanted me to go, so I just recited the most recent thing I'd done," he told her glibly. "Then said what I did before that, and then before that, and then—"

He was making her headache infinitely worse. "I get it, I get it," she snapped, holding her head.

Right now it felt as if her head was going to come off and from where she sat, it almost seemed like a blessing. She wasn't subjected to these pounding recitals of throbbing veins often, but they were excruciating when they hit, starting her morning with her and refusing to abate, sometimes for the duration of the whole day.

She'd been assured that these headaches weren't migraines, and that more than likely, tension was responsible for creating them. But knowing that—or at least being told that—didn't make the pain any easier to tolerate.

"Are you always this perverse in the morning?" she asked. As she spoke, she squeezed her eyes shut, trying vainly to block out the sunlight that came into the room.

"I like rising to a challenge," he cracked. He looked at her more closely. "What's wrong?"

She was not about to sit here and admit her pain. The man would probably use any excuse to make her drop out of whatever he was planning to do. "Nothing."

"Then why do you look as if your head might implode at any second?"

At this point, Tiana hurt far too much to pretend she didn't. Besides, what did it matter if he knew? It wasn't a disabling condition, just a very, very painful one. If he tried to use this as an excuse to make her stay here, out of his way, he was going to find out just how stubborn she could be. This headache made her far less tolerant and more inclined to speak her mind without pausing to choose the nicest phrasing.

"Because it might," she admitted.

"Headache?" he asked.

If she didn't know better, she would have said that he sounded almost sympathetic.

Tiana shifted on the sofa, trying to will herself to

get up—but that would require movement, and movement right now would only intensify this awful pain.

Maybe she could just wait it out. Even a few minutes might make some sort of a difference.

"Head-quake is more like it," she admitted.

"I take it this isn't the first time," he guessed.

She tried to shrug and stopped because that just seemed to add to the pain. "It happens," she admitted vaguely.

"Have you seen a doctor about it?" Brennan asked.

"I don't have a brain tumor if that's what you're wondering," she told him. "It's not even a migraine according to the specialist. He tells me it's just stress." Which, the way she saw it, was just a cop-out. "When in doubt, blame it on stress," she quipped, keeping her voice down low because almost anything above a whisper echoed inside her head and sent out long, scratchy fingers that poked absolutely everywhere.

"So technically, you're saying you need to destress?" Brennan asked.

"Yeah, that would be nice." She laughed softly at the very idea, considering the situation that they were dealing with. She opened her eyes just a slit. "Got any suggestions?"

To her surprise he said, "A couple."

She opened her eyes a little farther and raised them to his. They locked for a moment and she instantly guessed exactly what his first suggestion as to "destressing" entailed.

"Other than that," she told him. "If anything, something physical like that would probably make my head explode," she predicted.

Any sudden movement was really hard for her. How was she going to get ready? This pain she was experiencing was already lasting longer than most of her attacks, which struck hard, then faded into the background by inches. But if anything, this seemed to be getting stronger. Or at least remaining as strong as it had been to begin with.

What if it refused to abate? How was she going to be able to drive, to work with this man on trying to find a way to rescue her sister and the other girls?

A wave of angry despair washed over her.

Caught up in the web of pain that was relentlessly assaulting her, she didn't realize Brennan had circled behind her until she felt his fingertips lightly touching her temples on either side of her head.

"What are you doing?" she demanded, then winced because her own voice sounded too loud and caused the pain in her head to intensify exponentially.

"Shh," Brennan chided, then advised her to "Just relax."

"With you standing behind me like that?" she asked. "You're kidding, right?"

"No, I'm deadly serious," he said, his voice low, melodic and, despite the score of little men equipped with jackhammers pounding in her head, very nearly damn seductive. "Now do as I say," he told her. "Relax."

"I can't, I—"

Tiana didn't finish her protest because, startlingly enough, the tension began to leach away from her. Not in any large wave that left an instant impression on her, but in tiny yet noticeable increments.

First the tension receded from her toes, then her feet and slowly, from her ankles. Her lower legs were next, then her knees, her thighs and so on. It was a slow progression to the heart of her, working its way up her neck and face until it finally reached her temples, the origin of the pain and the only area that Brennan was touching.

His fingers worked along her temples in steady, concentric circles that acted almost like gently pulsating radio waves, reaching everything, working their magic where it was needed.

"Is it working?" Brennan asked after a few minutes, observing. "Because your shoulders no longer look as if you could land Boeing 747s on them. One of your shoulders is actually even drooping a little," he noted.

This was incredible. He had succeeded in making her feel human in an infinitely short amount of time. He'd succeeded where an emergency room physician had once failed.

"You didn't tell me you were part magician," she said to him.

"You didn't ask," he quipped.

She could almost *hear* him grin. Funny thing about it was, it didn't really bother her.

"Anything else I should ask that I didn't?" she asked, barely able to form words, he had her that relaxed.

"Maybe we'll get to that by and by, Venus," Brennan deadpanned.

"I should be worried, shouldn't I?" Tiana said, knowing that in order to keep strictly safe, she should be moving out of the range of those incredible fingers of his, but he was making her feel good again and she was afraid if she made him stop, all the pain would come rushing back, maybe even twice as bad as before. As far as she was concerned, he was working a miracle.

As he massaged her temples, Brennan had the strongest urge to slide his hands along the sides of her slender neck and onto her shoulders.

Be honest, man, that's not where you want your hands to stop and you know it.

Rousing himself, Brennan made himself focus on what she'd just said and not what he was feeling right now. "My mother used to say 'Don't borrow trouble. It'll find you soon enough.'"

"She sounds like a very wise lady."

Brennan stopped massaging her temples for a moment, remembering. Bits and pieces of his favorite memories came to him. His mother had died almost ten years ago and he still caught himself missing her fiercely at times. How much harder was it for his father? he couldn't help wondering.

"She was," he answered. And then he shook off the somber mood that threatened to envelop him and thought of the way his mother laughed. The sound was infectious. No one could ever keep a straight face when his mother laughed.

"You kind of remind me a little of her," he told Tiana. "She was just as stubborn as you are."

Was. He was using the past tense, she realized. So he didn't have a mother, either. That gave them one small thing in common, Tiana thought. *Don't get carried away. Lots of people don't have mothers. This doesn't mean anything.*

"I'm not stubborn," she protested, trying to look stern. "I just don't back down when I'm right—which I am most of the time," she added.

"Uh-huh," he said, humoring her.

He'd been massaging her temples for a while now and she could feel all the tension leaving her body. Very slowly, Brennan withdrew his fingers.

She felt the lack instantly. "Don't stop." It was as close to begging as she'd allow herself to get.

"If your headache is still there, I think we should see about getting you to the E.R. They've got to be able to give you something to help manage the pain," he told her. He waited for some sort of a response from her, but she didn't say a word. "Well?" he pressed.

Tiana turned in slow motion to look at him, an expression of sheer wonder on her face. It struck him at that moment that he'd never seen anything so beautiful in his life. The next moment, he forced himself to snap out of it, to focus on what was important, not beautiful. He had a mission to see through. What he was feeling right now had no part in it. If he lost sight of that, he was dead. They both were.

"It's gone," she whispered in complete wonder. The next moment, she repeated the words, this time more audibly. "It's gone." The increase in volume didn't make her wince. Unbelievable, she thought. "How did you *do* that?"

Before he could answer her, she'd reacted strictly out of relief and gratitude and thrown her arms around his neck. Overjoyed that the pain didn't return, she kissed him.

The next second, she realized what she'd done and began to pull back. But it was already too late. Because in that tiny space of time, Brennan had reacted and deepened the kiss that had begun so fleetingly. Once he did, she found herself being drawn to him. Strongly drawn. And the kiss that had begun as an automatic show of thanks flowered into something that was teeming with emotions, a passion she had been keeping under wraps for most of her life.

He wondered if she knew just how sweet her mouth was and how even this simple contact between them was causing all sorts of havoc to happen inside him. His line of work didn't leave any time for relationships. On the job they would have been formed in lies—not to mention that his last assignment had him posing as a homeless man who attracted flies more than women.

As for a relationship outside his line of work, what woman would have been satisfied with just crumbs tossed in her direction, with seeing him for snatches of time whenever he could safely get away?

He wasn't celibate. There'd been a few hookups, but none of those extended past a weekend. Two at most. He made sure of it.

This, however, didn't fall into that category.

This, he told himself, wasn't going to fall into

any category, because he'd just slipped up, nothing more. What he was experiencing right at this moment couldn't go anywhere. They were working together, and *that* was the only part that mattered.

Drawing away from her, he continued as if nothing had happened, although it was far from easy. "That's something I picked up from this woman I dated. The massaging-your-temples thing," he clarified when she looked at him with a dazed, puzzled expression. "She was into holistic medicine."

For a second, when he said he'd "picked this up" from a woman he'd dated, Tiana thought he was referring to kissing her. God, but he had practically caused her to incinerate right on the spot. She was going to have to watch herself. Another man would have taken complete advantage of the situation and of her. She didn't know whether to be grateful or upset that there was something about her that made him choose not to continue or let things progress naturally.

She cleared her throat and pretended to be completely unaffected by what had just happened. "Nice to know you're always trying to further your education."

"You're never too old to keep learning," he replied. His voice sounded just the slightest bit off to his own ear.

Before she could say anything in response, or comment further on his unique method of furthering his education, Brennan's phone began to buzz insistently. He picked it up and looked at the screen.

"I've got to take this," he told her, turning away. "It's Roland."

Chapter 11

Brennan walked across the room before he took the call. Since he had his back to her, Tiana couldn't hear any of the words, but she tried to gauge whether the call contained good news—by their standards—or bad by watching the set of Brennan's shoulders as he spoke to the man. She couldn't reach a conclusion.

The call was brief.

The second he ended it, Tiana hurried across the room to him immediately. "Was that actually Roland, or one of his henchmen?" she asked.

"It was Roland. How fast can you get ready?" Brennan asked her.

"Fast enough," she said, then gave him his due and added, "Thanks to you," referring to the fact that he had made her headache disappear and she didn't have to worry about every little movement bringing waves of pain with it.

Taking the suitcase that Brennan had brought up with them last night, she headed to the bathroom. She really would have loved to take a shower, but she sensed that there wasn't time for that. She settled for a change of clothes and splashing water in her face before freshening her makeup.

Through it all, she kept the door partially open so that she could talk to him.

"What's up?" she called out to him as she discarded what she was wearing and hurried into a fresh two-piece outfit, a formfitting, light blue-gray skirt and top that gave the illusion of a dress once on.

He knew by the sounds she was making that she was getting dressed. Brennan was tempted to draw closer to the bathroom to look in, or at least position himself so that he could see her reflected in the bathroom mirror. But with effort, he got his curiosity—and the temptation to satisfy it—sufficiently under control and gave her the space she needed to get ready.

However, his imagination was having a field day. Try as he might, there was nothing he could do to rein *that* in.

Answering her, he addressed his comments to the air between them.

"The timetable's been moved up. Roland had his men move the girls again to a new undisclosed location even though, rumor has it, they're supposed to be uprooting everyone in less than a week. He hinted that he's not averse to making money on the side by selling off some of his—as he put it—'inventory' before the rest of that 'inventory' is shipped to an undisclosed location—most likely out of the country."

Dressed, she came out, deftly twisting her hair behind her so that she could secure it up.

"So he'll let us see them?" Tiana asked eagerly, pushing the last pin in.

Brennan shook his head. "Not yet. He'll let us see the photographs."

Even if Janie was one of the girls in the photographs, that still wasn't good enough. Tiana needed to know where Janie was being held and if she was *currently* all right. "And if we insist on seeing the girls in the flesh?"

If they pushed too hard, that might backfire on them, Brennan thought. They needed to display just the right mixture of persuasion and pressure. And what accomplished that faster than anything else was cold, hard cash.

"That might depend on the amount of money we flash in front of him," Brennan responded, still looking off into space. "But it's certainly worth a shot."

"You can stop being noble, I'm dressed," she told him, circling around so that she was right in front of him. "All done," she announced.

He looked at her in surprise. She appeared ready to go. That had to be some sort of a female record as far as he knew. "That fast?" he asked, surprised.

"I was changing my clothes, not fighting my way out of a cocoon so I could 'magically' transform into a butterfly," she pointed out.

He shrugged indifferently at her explanation, only half hearing her. Even without makeup and under less than ideal conditions, she was beautiful. "It's just that the women I know take longer to brush their teeth than you just took to get ready."

"Maybe I just have smaller teeth," she quipped, the corners of her mouth curving appealingly.

"How's the headache?" he asked, pausing to do a quick check of his weapon before they left.

Brennan made certain his gun was in prime condition because there was a lot riding on how quickly he might have to fire it. He had to go through the motions of checking it at the door with Roland's gatekeeper, but as long as it was somewhere in the vicinity, he wanted it primed and ready to fire.

"Completely gone, thanks to you." She still found that rather awesome. "You know, if this gig with the police department doesn't work out for you, you can always fall back on giving massages. I'm sure that a lot of people would be willing to have you name your own price if you could help them as quickly as you helped me."

"As flattering as that sounds, I'm pretty certain I can make this gig work," he told her, humor curving his rather generous mouth. "You want to stop to get a bite?" he suggested as they walked out of the room together. He paused a second to test the door, making sure that it was locked.

"We can get it to go," she suggested. "Can't keep the boss man or his ego waiting."

There was no arguing with that, but even so, Brennan caught her arm just as she began to walk to the nearest bank of elevators. "Are you sure you're up to this?" he asked.

She would never have pegged him for a mother hen, she thought. "I told you, thanks to you, the headache's gone, like it never even existed."

He shook his head. "I wasn't talking about the headache."

Tiana frowned. She didn't understand. "Then what?" she asked.

They were heading into very emotional territory. He had to know if she could keep her feelings from registering on her face. They couldn't afford to arouse any suspicions as to their real purpose in all this. She might act like some tough, stubborn little cookie, but he was certain that Roland had ways of breaking people. And if he was the slightest bit doubtful that she— or he—weren't who they said they were, this could all go down very badly very quickly.

"Are you sure you can handle seeing a photograph of your sister?" he asked. "Or worse, *not* seeing a photograph of your sister?"

She knew the implication in the latter scenario was that her sister either was dead or had already been shipped out. She'd already entertained that scenario and was prepared for it even as she fervently hoped it wouldn't come to pass.

"Look, I'm not some civilian off the street," she reminded him patiently. "I'm a crime scene investigator who's been at this for a few years now. Yes, I'm emotionally involved, but I also know what happens if that emotion is detected or, worse, gets the better of me. I'm here to rescue Janie and as many other girls as I can. I'm not here to wring my hands, break down sobbing and expect other people to do my job for me. Are we clear?" she asked.

For one moment, it seemed to him that she was behaving as if their roles were reversed. That probably wasn't her intention. She wasn't here to make any points or further her career. She wasn't even trying to successfully conclude an assignment, the way he was. This woman was here for exactly the reason she had just said: to rescue her sister. And she was singularly focused on her goal.

He wasn't giving the woman her due, Brennan thought, wasn't treating her like the professional she was—just as much of a professional as he was, he judged. Her commitment just came wrapped in a more identifiable package.

He nodded in response to her statement. "Okay, then, let's go." The elevator opened its doors almost the moment he pushed the down button. He gestured for her to enter.

So he wasn't going to try to argue her out of coming with him, Tiana thought in relief. "Good, because after all you've done for me, I would hate to have to knock you out and leave you behind because you're determined to make me wait this dance out."

Brennan laughed. He had a feeling that she was deadly serious. "Another thing my mother did—she didn't raise any stupid children."

Her smile was warm and genuine and just for a

moment, she let her guard down as she told Brennan, "I'd say that your mother is beginning to sound like one hell of a lady."

"She was," he agreed. He felt an all too familiar wave of sorrow washing over him as the memory of his mother echoed through him. "And she would have liked you a lot."

"Okay, then let's both do her proud and catch this flesh peddling SOB."

"*And* the man he takes orders from," he reminded her just as they reached the ground floor.

Damn, she'd just about forgotten about that, Tiana thought as they got out and made their way through the hotel lobby. This was another large bump in the road. Large enough to prove to be an obstacle.

She couldn't think about it now. They'd tackle that problem when the time came, she promised herself.

At this particular moment, there was nothing else she could do.

As before, both he and Tiana passed beneath the watchful eyes of Roland's behemoth of a security guard and his two hulking bodyguards.

"They give me the creeps," Tiana told Brennan in a low voice.

"They're supposed to," he guessed.

"Well, then they're doing a bang-up job," she confided.

And then they were ushered in for an audience with the highest man in the organization they were allowed to deal with—for the time being.

Isaac Roland looked as if he was studying to become a world-class dictator, Tiana thought. She preferred the bodyguards who appeared more honest in what they were all about. Their job was to protect this poor excuse for a human being, and one look at them told her they intended to do whatever it took to accomplish that goal. She also saw that they didn't like the man, but then, they weren't being paid to like him. They were being paid to protect him, which they were honor-bound to do.

And for his part, she had a feeling that Roland would have had them cut down in a minute if it suited his purpose. Tiana could just *feel* that in her gut.

The would-be-kingpin assessed them, his green eyes cold and unfathomable even though he had a smile on his thin lips. "I trust you both spent a good night and that it only sharpened your appetites for what I have to offer."

"We initially came here wanting what you had to offer," Brennan patiently reminded the man, speaking to him with the professed affection that someone might demonstrate to an eccentric but favored uncle.

"Yes, but waiting always heightens the anticipation, don't you think?"

No doubt, it wasn't a question he expected an answer to. Instead, Roland snapped his fingers at one of his two bodyguards, indicating that he wanted the man to fetch something.

The man, already informed as to what he was to bring, inclined his head and all but left the room walking backward.

Tiana had a hunch that the man's obsequious behavior had to do with the bodyguard sensing that he
was going to be out of a job soon as far as the higher
levels were concerned. That meant that he needed to
ingratiate himself to Roland before it was too late and
he was turned out on the street.

Within a minute, if not less, the hulking bodyguard
returned with a rather large bound portfolio. The item
turned out to be filled to capacity and then some with
photographs of the girls Roland currently had in his
possession.

Roland indicated that the bodyguard should hand
the portfolio to Brennan, which he did. The reed-thin
man gestured toward the pristine white sofa.

"Sit, look, decide," he urged them both in a mag-
nanimous tone befitting a benefactor rather than a man
who dealt with the sale of human flesh.

Tiana pretended to glance at the first photograph
in the collection. She looked at it just long enough to
ascertain that it wasn't Janie.

"It's easy to retouch photographs," she told Roland.
"I'd have to see the girls in person before I paid any
money for them, especially the top dollar you're charg-
ing." Her eyes met his when he raised them. Tapping
into inner resolve, she refused to look away. If she did,
then he would have won.

He still might, Tiana warned herself. The man was
like a dangerous copperhead. You just never looked
away, thinking yourself safe. That was when the snake
struck, delivering a deadly bite.

"I have only the best quality to offer," Roland countered. "These girls are worth every penny I charge for them," he insisted, his smile never wavering. It also never reached his eyes. "They are young enough to fulfill anyone's fantasy and old enough to be experienced at what they're doing."

She wanted to call him a liar, because her sister was supposedly in that group he was parading around for prospective buyers and she was so innocent and so inexperienced, the horror of what she was expected to do—what she *had* to do in order to survive—would either push Janie off the deep end—or wind up killing her one way or another.

But in order not to blow their cover and to stay in this vital life-or-death game, Tiana couldn't allow herself to dwell on any of that.

Instead, Tiana told the man she regarded as a reptilian creature in a suit what she felt a woman her age, and of the mind-set she'd put forth, would say in her situation.

"They sound good on paper, but I still have to see them in person, or there's no deal."

Roland sighed, an emperor struggling not to bring his fist down on a pesky insect. "All right, fair enough. I've got a couple of days' leeway yet," he said, which was the closest he'd alluded to having to transfer the girls from their present location. "You make your choices and we'll see about arranging some sort of viewing for you. Although I guarantee that any girl you pick is going to more than live up to whatever standards you've set for these lost souls."

It took everything she had not to throw up right then

and there. "And you're what? The Good Shepherd?" she challenged, unable to restrain herself.

"The Good Shepherd," Roland repeated, as if trying the identity on for size. "I rather like that," he told her with a nod of approval. "I hadn't thought of it as that before you said it, but yes, I suppose I am these girls' Good Shepherd at that." He watched her intently, a leer taking command over his features. Then, to both her and Brennan's surprise, Roland's eyes narrowed to slits and he roughly took hold of her chin in his hand, his eyes taunting hers. "You want to come worship at my feet?" he proposed with a laugh that was border-line maniacal.

That cinched it for her, Tiana thought. The man was certifiably crazy.

Because Roland was apparently waiting for an answer to his absurd question, she told him, "Later, once I have the girls I need for my business, then we'll see," doing what she could to play up the attraction angle between them even as the very hint of the idea turned her stomach and threatened to have her purging every last ounce of breakfast.

Roland gestured toward the portfolio that was currently in Brennan's possession. "Keep looking," he all but ordered her. "They're not in any particular order, yet there should be several in that batch that'll get your clock ticking," he promised.

"You have the girls' ages entered on the back of the photograph?" she asked as she settled on the sofa with the portfolio across her knee.

It was obvious that Roland saw no point to asking for the information.

"What for? Half of them would lie about it. Usually can't get a straight answer out of a broad about her birthday, anyway." He laughed harshly. "But just try forgetting it," he murmured under his breath, and it seemed apparent that what the trafficker was referring to had transpired relatively recently.

Was the man actually married? Did he have children? The concept seemed too absurd to contemplate, given his chosen vocation. But then, it had been known to happen more than once. A family could provide the kind of cover a man in his line of "work" might very well need.

"All right, sit down and start looking before I change my mind and have you out on your asses. Both of you," he stressed. "That means you, too, pretty boy," Roland said mockingly. He was clearly jealous of the fact that the man who had brought her to him was far handsomer than he was or had ever been.

Before she and Brennan got back to looking through the portfolio, Tiana raised her voice—so he could hear her—and asked, "Are there any more portfolios?"

Roland turned around and eyed her incredulously. "Why?" he asked. "You finish looking through those already?" He jeered. They all knew it was physically impossible to have gone through a quarter of the photographs in such a short space of time, much less all of them.

She forced herself to treat what he'd just said as a legitimate question. It was far harder than it might seem, given that she wanted desperately to smash something into his sneering face.

"No, I was just wondering if this was the only one or if there were more—in case I wanted to expand my operation even further."

"There's always more," Roland told her cryptically. "Get through that one and we'll see what's available to you. When did someone in your line of work get so damn picky?" he asked.

"I don't know about someone else," she replied evenly, "but as for me, I've always been picky. You and I haven't done business before, so you would really have no reason to know how I feel about anything, especially my girls."

Roland nodded, as if he agreed with what she was telling him. "Fair enough."

But even as he said it, she sensed that the living embodiment of an egomaniac did *not* like being talked to as if he were an ordinary person, capable of making mistakes.

She'd just made a tactical error.

Somewhere, on some imaginary chalkboard, there was a black mark beside her name.

Roland went into another room busying himself with his affairs, and she and Brennan got down to work.

Tiana found it almost physically challenging to keep her hand from trembling as she looked at each photograph, then turned it facedown on a pile.

This wasn't a pile of photographs; these were people. Frightened, damaged and emotionally scarred children even if they had the bodies of women. Her heart ached for each and every one of them.

They had to find out where those girls were being kept—they *had* to. If they didn't free them, she wouldn't be able to sleep a wink for the rest of her life.

Inwardly, all of her was shaking. That made it difficult for her not to keep a cool head. If she let slip her horror, if even one *hint* of what she and Brennan were up to got out, it would jeopardize the entire operation—not to mention it would kill any chances she had of rescuing Janie.

Possibly kill them, as well.

So willing herself to be calm for Janie's sake, Tiana slowly turned the pages of the portfolio Roland had provided, doing her best not to allow her stomach to rise to her throat as she looked at the faces of desolation and hopelessness in fancy, revealing dresses.

She was certain that at least half the girls she was looking at had given up hope of going back to their homes again.

A closer examination of the faces allowed her to see that a great many of the girls appeared oddly complacent, wearing the same vacant expressions of girls who had been deliberately drugged and couldn't quite fathom what was happening around them and *to* them.

Until they were raped.

Or worse.

After fifteen agonizing minutes of looking very closely at every single photograph in the portfolio, Tiana closed it.

Janie wasn't among the faces.

Chapter 12

"Well?" Roland asked expectantly the moment he saw that she had closed the portfolio.

Brennan took over. "Not a bad selection," he said, speaking for both of them. "But I'd like to see more before I make up my mind."

"A discerning man." Roland's tone had more than just a touch of mocking in it. "Sure, why not?"

Turning to the bodyguard who had brought out the first collection of photographs, Roland snapped his fingers, indicating he wanted the man to fetch another portfolio.

Tiana could see that Roland enjoyed playing dictator as much as the bodyguard hated having to go along with playing the man's servant.

"You know," Tiana once again pointed out to Roland, "this could go a whole lot quicker if we could see the girls in person."

"I'm sure it would," Roland replied coolly. The moment the bodyguard reappeared, he took the new portfolio from him and passed the bound collection over to Brennan.

"Well, then?" Brennan asked, holding on to the portfolio but not bothering to open it yet. "Why don't we go see them?"

Roland's eyes narrowed into dark slits. Tiana couldn't help thinking that it made him look every inch of the snake that he reminded her of.

"We'll go see the merchandise when *I* say we see them, not when you say so." Roland paused for a moment, then added dramatically, "Understand?"

Brennan decided to push the man a little further toward the edge. He did not look like someone who held on to his temper well. Losing his cool just might get Roland to say something he hadn't intended to let slip.

"What's the matter, boss man won't let you make an independent decision without consulting him first?" he guessed.

Brennan had pushed the right buttons—or the wrong ones, depending on which point of view was being taken.

"What the hell are you talking about?" Roland demanded hotly. He jerked a thumb at his own chest. "I'm the boss man."

"In this room, yes, I agree," Brennan continued, speaking so amiably, he might as well have been talking about something as innocuous as a new kind of salad dressing. "But in the organization, there's someone else running the show, isn't there?"

Roland clearly had his back up. "You asking me or telling me?" the older man asked malevolently.

"Telling," Brennan responded mildly. "Hey, no offense intended, but something that large, with connections in other states, not to mention maybe even other countries, that takes someone who moves around in larger circles than this. You might very well be in charge of this area, but someone else calls the shots," Brennan maintained.

She could see that Brennan was getting to the other man. For the most part, she'd let the scenario play itself out in front of her while she observed both participants closely as well as the two men in the background. She could tell by the veiled expressions on the two bodyguards' faces that Roland might be the one they interacted with directly and he was the one they guarded, the one who paid their salaries. But it was also obvious—at least to her—that they were rooting for Brennan all the way.

Tiana couldn't help wondering what it would take to turn the men. She had a hunch that something as simple as the promise of immunity in exchange for useful information against Roland would be the way to get the two giants to sing like overweight canaries.

"There's no shame in taking orders from someone higher up," Brennan was saying as Roland's face began to turn a bright shade of red. There was definitely nothing suppressed about the man's anger, Tiana thought. "We all do it. I know that I do. Even our little high and mighty madam here—" he gestured toward her "—answers to someone. Don't you, sweetheart?"

"I might," she agreed, taking her cue from Brennan and being deliberately vague. "But one thing's for damn sure. I'm not your 'sweetheart.'"

Out of the corner of her eye she saw that Roland liked her putting "Wayne" down—just as she thought he might. She was about to comment further when something in her peripheral vision caused her heart to suddenly lodge itself in her throat. She'd been paging through the second portfolio, only half glancing at each photograph she turned to when she saw her.

Saw her sister.

Saw Janie.

Suddenly, the room darkened just for a moment while her head felt as if it was pulsating wildly.

She looked down at the photograph. They had her sister dressed in some outlandish, incredibly tight dress that was cut too low on top and cut way too high at the bottom. What her sister had been forced to wear was hardly little more than a tight, hot-pink Band-Aid.

Janie had always hated the color pink.

Strange the thoughts that went through your head when you were coming unglued.

Roland laughed, pleased with the fact that the madam was obviously turning on the other man. "Looks like you're on your own here, Wayne."

She looked up at Roland, secretly marveling at the fact that she could still keep a civil tongue in her head. She would have thought that by now she would have thrown a noose around the smug man's neck and threatened him with extreme bodily harm unless he gave her the exact location where the girls were being kept prisoner. Tiana struggled to get herself under control. Losing her temper like that would only put her—and Cavanaugh—in danger.

Taking a deep breath, she set Roland straight. "Actually, I'm with the pretty boy on this one. Like I already said before, making our selections in person would be a lot easier than looking at eight-by-ten glossies that might have been retouched."

"Why the hell do you keep harping on that? Nobody retouched anything," Roland retorted angrily. "As for going on that little field trip you keep obsessing about—when the time's right, you'll be notified where the girls are staying. Right now, if you see anything you like, let me know. I'll see to it that those girls aren't shipped off until you get to see them, in the flesh." Then, because he realized what he'd said, Roland laughed. Coming from him, the sound came across as sardonic.

God help her, she didn't trust a single thing coming out of the smarmy man's mouth. She had the feeling that he was just saying anything that came to mind in order to get her to play along.

"Fair enough," she replied, grinding out the words through gritted teeth. She quickly pulled the so-called candidates on her "wish list." There were ten photographs in all and she handed them over to Roland.

The man didn't really look through the batch. He counted the number. It was obvious that he thought the total was too low.

"Just ten?" he demanded. "Out of two portfolios, that's all you can come up with?"

"I might want more once I see them in person," she allowed, "but right now those are the only ones who make the grade."

"You haven't looked through the third portfolio," the older man pointed out, sparing a glance toward "Wayne," as well.

"Then let me see it," she told him. But when Roland went to take the portfolio from her, she cried, "Wait," then turned toward Brennan and asked, "You want to look through these again?"

"I'm done. I've got to say," he said loftily to Roland, "I'm not all that impressed. I hope the ones in the next batch have something more going for them than the ones I've seen so far."

"What's wrong with them?" Roland retorted angrily.

"It's not a matter of there being anything 'wrong' with them so much as there's nothing special about these girls. There's no spark. They certainly don't look as if they would light up a room—or that they're worth your asking price."

That goaded Roland. It was obvious that he took any derogatory remarks made about his inventory personally. "Get the third portfolio," he ordered his man.

"You'll want to put these back," Tiana said, referring to the two giant folders that were beside her on the sofa.

Getting up, she took a few steps toward Roland in order to hand over both collections. She suddenly stumbled, her heel appearing to have gotten caught on the edge of the decorative Persian rug that ran the length of the sofa. It looked as if she was going to fall right in front of him had Roland not automatically reached out to catch her.

Tiana cried out as she dropped the folders but managed to catch hold of Roland's thin shoulders to steady herself.

"Oh, I'm sorry, I didn't mean to drop them," she said. Photographs were scattered in every direction. She went through the motions of sinking down to gather together the portfolio's spilled contents, but Roland grabbed her hand and yanked her back up to her feet.

"Well, don't just stand there, pick them up," he barked the order at the two bodyguards.

The two lumbered over, gracelessly bending over to retrieve the photographs. It was impossible to tell which belonged to what portfolio.

"I'm so sorry," Tiana apologized again.

Roland was quick to dismiss the need for an apology. "No harm done. Are you okay?" he asked solicitously. "You didn't pull anything, did you? I could check you over to make sure," he offered with an unabashed leer.

Brennan noticed that she still had one hand on the other man's shoulder as she appeared to steady herself. "No, no, I'm fine. My heel just got caught on the edge of that rug. Lucky for me, you were there to break my fall, otherwise I'd be covered with bruises by tomorrow morning." She smiled warmly at him. "Thanks for being my guardian angel."

"No problem," Roland assured her magnanimously. "Do you feel up to going through the last batch of photographs?"

She couldn't help wondering what sort of fragile women he encountered in his world. Maybe they used anything as an excuse to appear incapacitated. Dealing with the man, she didn't wonder at their motivation.

"Of course," she answered, smiling brightly. "That's why I'm here."

Viewing the last batch of photographs went rather quickly. She already had what she wanted, confirmation that Janie was here. Part of her wanted to cut through the pretense and put a gun to Roland's head, demanding to know where Janie was being kept right now.

But doing that wouldn't give them what Brennan was after, and if the man in charge of the organization wounded up escaping, all this would wind up happening again in other towns and cities to other unsuspecting girls, turning their existence into a hell on earth and bringing agony to their families.

So she went through the motions and prayed this would all be over with soon. She was doing her part in all this to make that happen.

Between Brennan and her, they had "preselected" thirty-five girls. Girls, they made it clear, they expected to see in person. They both remained adamant on that salient point. They wanted to "see the merchandise" before paying for it.

Roland promised to make some calls to put things in motion once they had left and then said he would get back to them. He might have said "them," but he was only looking at Tiana when he made the promise.

They were dismissed from the hotel suite and sent on their way, just as they had been the last time. Roland was still playing dictator.

Brennan waited until they were well clear of Roland's hotel and in his car, on their way back to his hotel before he asked, "What are you up to?"

"I already told you. Getting my sister back."

Janie wasn't as tough as she was, Tiana told herself. But she could survive this ordeal, not let it define her—or at least she fervently hoped that was the case. But she also knew that it was just a matter of time before her sister broke down. She had to get her out before then. At the very least, she had to let her sister know she was working on her rescue.

"You know what I'm talking about," Brennan told her. "What was with that 'oops, I'm falling' act back in the suite?"

She turned toward him, the face of innocence. "What, don't people trip in your world? Or are they all surefooted goats?"

"You didn't look like you tripped," he told her. "You looked like you pitched forward."

"The difference being?" she asked innocently, leaving the end of her sentence up in the air.

"The difference being that one happens naturally and the other is staged."

She laughed at his assessment. He'd caught on, but

then, the man had struck her as being brighter than the average person right from the beginning. "Well, hopefully, Roland isn't as astute as you are."

Brennan laughed shortly, dismissing the compliment. After getting to know him a little, he thought of Roland as being only slightly smarter than a single-cell amoeba. "From where I was standing, Roland looked happy just to have an excuse to grab you. Frankly, he seemed to be hoping your clothes were going to fall off next."

"Yeah, well, he can hope all he wants to. It's not going to happen," Tiana said firmly, adding, "Not for *any* reason."

They'd arrived at the hotel and he got out, allowing the valet to take his car and park it for him. "Tripping is a diversion," he said, looking at her and waiting for an explanation.

"It can be," she agreed, walking ahead of him into the hotel.

Once inside, she kept walking. He had to speed up his pace in order to catch up.

Since she wasn't elaborating any further on her own, he asked, "Exactly what were you diverting his attention from?"

"You skip the class on English grammar?" she asked, amused. "That is one awful sentence."

He enjoyed wordplay as much as the next person, but he'd been patient long enough. "Stop stalling and answer the question."

She inclined her head, lowering her voice at the same time so that only he could hear what she was saying. "You said yourself that we can't move in until we know who's calling the shots, right?"

His eyes never left her face. "Right."

"Well, since we made our selections, and Roland apparently doesn't do anything more independent than get dressed by himself, he's going to have to call whoever is heading this operation to ask for the go-ahead to bring us to where the girls are being kept."

"With you so far," Brennan said, doing his best to remain patient. He could see that she was enjoying herself, drawing this out. Considering what she'd been through already, he let her have her moment—but he was determined that it would only be the one.

"If we record Roland's conversation when he calls his boss, didn't you mention that there was an IT wizard back at your CSI lab who could track down the IP connection and get a name?"

"Yes." Brennan drew out the single word, still waiting.

"What would you say if I told you that I planted a minitransmitter on Roland's person that can pick up every conversation he has, whether in person or over the phone?"

He stared at her. "I'd say how the hell did you manage to do that?"

"I slipped it under his collar when I made a grab for him to supposedly keep from doing a face-plant on the floor in his hotel suite. As far as he was concerned, he was getting his jollies holding me against him. He had no idea what I was doing."

To say he was surprised would have been understating the matter. "But I saw you. You hardly touched him."

She merely grinned with satisfaction. "Doesn't take long if you know what you're doing and how to do it."

"And you know how to do it." It wasn't a question so much as it was a statement underscored with admiration.

Again she inclined her head, this time as if she was humbly taking a bow. "I do."

He was impressed. "Where did you pick up that little trick?"

"That's exactly what it is, a trick. A magic trick," she specified. "When I was growing up, my dad had a friend on the force, Ray Holland. Ray's hobby was doing magic tricks. Janie and I were his very attentive audience. He was kind of a lonely man, didn't have much luck with women," she recalled. "We were always happy to see him when he came by to dinner and he showed his gratitude by teaching us a few basic tricks," she told him. "Janie and I practiced on each other," she recalled with a fond smile.

Brennan could only laugh as he shook his head. "You know, the longer I know you, the more interesting you become."

Having ridden up an empty elevator, they got off on their floor. "Is that a compliment?" she asked him.

"That is an observation," he replied honestly. "But you can take it as a compliment if you want. Just where did you get this microdigital camera?"

"I like keeping up on technology in my line of work," she told him casually.

Sliding his card through the door slot, he unlocked the hotel room, then let her walk in first.

At first glance, everything appeared just as they had left it. "Okay, so he had this transmitter attached to his person. What's next?"

"We take my monitoring equipment, go back to the vicinity of his hotel and park somewhere across the street—and hope we pick up some kind of pertinent information from him soon."

Taking her suitcase from under the bed where she had slid it earlier, she placed it on top and flipped open the locks. The monitor she was referring to was barely the size of a cell phone and looked very much like one, as well. After slipping it into her pocket, she dropped the glib act and looked at him, the smile gone from her eyes, replaced by concern and a sense of urgency.

"That monster's got Janie. I've got to get her out of there. I have this *really* bad feeling that if we don't—" She couldn't get herself to say it, to give voice to the dark thoughts that were ricocheting through her brain, all centering on the possibility that something awful was about to happen.

Tears shimmered in her eyes, tears that instantly hit him where he lived. Tears that made him want to do anything to wipe away their existence.

"But we will," he assured her. "We'll get to your sister and all the other girls in time. I promise."

As much as she wanted to believe him, she shook her head. "It's not in your power to promise something like that."

Placing his hand beneath her chin, he raised her

head so that her eyes met his. With the edge of his thumb, he wiped away some of her tears. At the same time, he looked into her eyes and repeated, "I promise," with quiet feeling and conviction.

And just like that, she found herself loving Brennan for that. For lying to her because she needed so badly to believe that everything was going to work out.

Chapter 13

*L*oving Brennan.

The thought, the singular *word,* telegraphing itself through her head out of the blue like that, rendered her utterly speechless for a moment.

Loving?

Really? What was going on with her?

She and the word *love* weren't even on a fleeting, nodding acquaintance level. Aside from Janie, she had never said or even *felt* that she loved anyone. Oh, she'd felt a filial type loyalty to her parents, even after they continued to disappoint her time and again. But whenever she looked back on her life with any measure of honesty, Tiana couldn't really say that she recalled *loving* either her mother or her father. They were family and she would have done things for them if the occasion or the necessity arouse, but that was out of a sense of obligation and duty, not because she loved either one of them. They weren't lovable.

They had, each in their own way, conducted a scorched-earth policy on her ability to love them—or, eventually, to be able to love anyone but Janie.

And yet there was definitely an effusion of emotion racing through her, overwhelming her right now. A lovely nervousness, for lack of a better word, that had seized her. Filling her with vague, delicious anticipation that remained formless, but there nonetheless.

Maybe it was just gratitude taken to the nth degree, Tiana thought. She really couldn't say for sure. All she knew was that she hadn't really felt whatever she was feeling at the moment *ever* before.

Because it made her nervous, Tiana tried to reason herself out of what she was thinking and feeling. Maybe she was just overwrought and emotionally exhausted. This certainly wasn't a state she was accustomed to or even vaguely familiar with.

Neither was this desire to be held, to be comforted, to gain some sort of emotional support. But there was no denying that she was very, very weary of constantly being strong, of only having herself to lean on, which was, at times, pretty much an emotionally exhausting endeavor.

She slanted a glance toward Brennan.

The way he was looking at her made her feel that he knew what she was thinking, what she was feeling and the remote possibility that he actually *might* know embarrassed her almost to pieces.

This flustered, fluttery person wasn't who she felt she was, or at least, it wasn't the face she wanted to present to the world. Weak people were looked down on, trampled on without so much as a backward glance or an afterthought. She couldn't allow herself to be that person no matter how weary she felt at times. If anything, she'd wind up hating herself, hating her spineless behavior.

"You know," Brennan was saying in the same quiet, understanding voice, "you don't have to shoulder all this all alone."

He *had* guessed what she was thinking, she thought, surprised. Not only that, but for a second she was *so* tempted to take him up on what he was hinting at—to share some of her burden with him.

Tiana did her best to shake off her desire to let him help. If nothing else, it just wasn't right to have him shoulder this with her. She hardly knew him.

And when this was over, he'd disappear out of her life—which would make everything that much worse. She *couldn't* let herself rely on him, or need him in any fashion. That was *not* something she could allow herself to get used to.

"Why, are you offering to adopt me?" Tiana quipped.

"And you don't have to joke in order to keep me at arm's length," he told her. "There's no shame in letting your guard down once in a while, no shame in needing help."

She squared her shoulders, refusing to give in, to admit he'd seen her for what she really was. "I don't need—"

She didn't get a chance to finish. Because he was attempting to get through to her via another route, to make her see that there was nothing wrong with being a little vulnerable and admitting it, because it made her human—and approachable.

"That's what teamwork is all about. Having each other's backs. *Helping* each other," Brennan deliberately emphasized.

She looked at him for a long moment. "You want to help me?" she finally asked.

There was no fanfare, no bravado in his answer. "Yes."

She pressed her lips together, then finally said, "Then stop being so nice to me."

Brennan laughed softly at her earnestly worded request, shaking his head. "You're complicated, I'll give you that."

She released the breath she was holding and crossed over to the hotel door ahead of Brennan. "Now that *that's* settled, let's go. We've got a lowlife to trap," she said gamely.

Twenty-four hours later, they were no further along than they had been when they set out. They had been in Brennan's car, parked a block away from the hotel's entrance, watching and listening to what amounted to utter nonsense, occasional strings of foul, bordering-on-obscene language and long stretches of silence intermittently sprinkled with sights and sounds of absolutely no consequence or interest.

It was like being tuned in to the world's most boring reality program, Tiana thought. She'd been so very on edge, waiting for something to break, that she was bordering on utter exhaustion.

What was glaringly missing was mention of anything even remotely related to the girls who were being held captive.

Roland, who slept late, drank and ate to excess, seemed content to just wait things out. His demeanor was such that she was fairly convinced he was into some sort of drug abuse off camera.

Either that or he was waiting them out.

"Think he's onto us?" she asked Brennan out of the blue.

She didn't know if she could take another five minutes of watching the monitor mounted inside Brennan's car. The one she'd handily hooked up in his vehicle once she'd planted it. And she needed to get out quick.

"No, despite what he might think of himself, he definitely isn't clever enough to plan something so subtle," he told her, looking away from the monitor that, because of where she had planted one of the transmitters, allowed for two alternating views of the main room. "I think he's just waiting it out because that was what he was told to do."

She found herself agreeing with Brennan's assessment. "Okay, then I have another question for you."

He glanced in her direction again—she was a lot easier on the eyes than the man on the screen they were supposed to be watching. "Go ahead."

"How do you keep parts of your body from going numb?" When Brennan gave her a grin that went a long way in making her stomach do some very strange things, Tiana immediately became more specific. "I mean like your legs and your butt."

"Oh, *those* parts." The wattage from his grin decreased a little. "Mind over matter," he told her. "Also getting out of the car and stretching a bit helps. You can take the next food run," he told her. "That coffee shop on the next corner," he pointed out, "also has a bathroom in the back should you find yourself needing one. And before you say you don't," he warned, way ahead of her, "even camels go once in a while."

She shrugged, dismissing his suggestion as unnecessary. "Not if they don't drink anything."

"That creates a whole host of other problems." He looked at her for a long moment, as if weighing the pros and cons of the situation. "I think we should take a break for a while."

She glared at him, appalled at the idea. What was he suggesting? This wasn't some game they could pause and return to later. "We can't pack it in now. We walk away, that'll be *just* when he places his call."

"I didn't say anything about packing it in," Brennan pointed out.

Her brow furrowed as she looked at him. Okay, he hadn't used those exact words, but that was the intent—wasn't it? "But you just said—"

There was no point in her finishing her sentence. "We're going to be spelled for a while," he said, cutting in.

As far as she knew, they were the only two working the case on this end. And she was here because she'd horned her way in. So what was he talking about? "Spelled by whom?"

The words were no sooner out of her mouth than Brennan nodded toward someone standing on her side of the vehicle. "By him," he prompted, indicating the person directly behind her.

The next moment, as she turned to look, the person Brennan was referring to crouched down to her level and look into the car. She quickly rolled down her window.

"My brother's not much on introductions," the casually dressed man with the infectious grin told her. "Hi, I'm Duncan and I'm here so that the two of you can get some shut-eye."

She glanced back at Brennan. "You called your brother?" she questioned.

"I called one of them," Brennan corrected. "Duncan was free and as it so happens, he owes me a favor." He offered her a bit more information. "Duncan's just transferred to the APD, same as me. And in case you're wondering, this has all been sanctioned by the chief of Ds," he assured her.

"When?" Tiana asked. Not that she didn't believe him, but as far as she knew, he hadn't had time to make any calls. They'd been together for the whole time. "We've been out on stakeout since yesterday."

"The chief knows how to read texts—and how to send them, as well," he told her. "Don't worry, nobody wants to do anything to jeopardize this assignment."

"Look, why don't you go?" she suggested to Brennan. He obviously wanted to get some sleep, and she didn't blame him in the slightest. But for him, this was just a case he was assigned to—for her, it was extremely personal. She needed to stay. "I'm fine."

"Is that so?" he asked skeptically. "Is that why you fell asleep twice in the last hour right in the middle of talking?"

"I did not," she cried indignantly. Then, because she wasn't nearly as sure as she was trying to pretend, she looked at him and asked, "Did I?"

"I wouldn't say it if it wasn't true," he pointed out simply. "Where's your car, Duncan?" he asked, looking over Tiana's shoulder at his brother.

"Parked half a block behind you. Oh, and Valri's coming, too." he said as an afterthought.

"Valri?" Tiana asked, looking from one brother to the other.

"One of our sisters," Duncan clarified before Brennan had the chance.

"You met her when you 'brought' me into the station. She was the one in uniform who gave me lip for not telling you who I was," he reminded her.

She remembered now. However, maybe it was lack of sleep, but she felt suddenly overwhelmed and outnumbered. It felt as if there were Cavanaughs coming out of the walls.

"How many of you are there?" she asked.

"Too many to tell you about right now," Brennan assured her. Getting out, he put his hand out to his younger brother. "Give me your keys. I'll bring your car back in a few hours."

"No problem," Duncan answered, handing over a

ring of keys. "You might want to fill it with gas if you get the chance," he added casually.

"Nothing would give me greater pleasure," Brennan answered sarcastically. Duncan had a bad habit of allowing gas tanks to become rather depleted when in his use.

"I know, that's why I didn't bother getting any before I came," Duncan deadpanned. "I knew you'd want to be the one to do it."

Rather than comment, Brennan turned his attention to the woman he'd been partnered with. The woman whose scent he'd been inhaling—with dizzying effects—these past twenty-four hours.

Opening the door on her side, he took hold of her arm. "C'mon, let's get you back to the hotel," Brennan coaxed, helping her out of the vehicle.

"The second you hear anything useful," she instructed Duncan solemnly, "call."

He nodded, knowing to keep a smile from surfacing. This wasn't his first rodeo, but Duncan allowed the woman with his brother to treat him as if he were a rookie. "You have my word."

"He's reliable, right?" she asked Brennan after they left Duncan in the surveillance car and walked away.

"He might look more like a kid than a man," Brennan told her, guessing at the source of her uneasiness, "but don't let that fool you. Duncan's extremely reliable. I wouldn't have asked him to take over the stakeout for a few hours if he wasn't. It's not like he's the only one available for the job," he added.

He stopped by his brother's vehicle and hit the security lock on the key ring. Four locks popped up simultaneously.

Tiana watched him over the roof of the sedan as she pulled the passenger-side door open. "Just how many do you have?"

He wasn't quite sure what she was asking. "Brothers? Or siblings?"

Getting in, she buckled up. "Siblings, I guess."

His seat belt fastened, Brennan started up the vehicle. The engine quietly purred to life. "Three brothers, three sisters."

She nodded in response to his answer. They pulled away from the curb, passing Duncan on the way back to their hotel. "Big family."

He laughed at her comment. "You don't know the half of it."

"Tell me," Tiana urged, curious what had made him laugh.

He recalled the recent changes in dynamics. He'd thought he had a large family before. Now it felt almost like being part of some kind of dynasty. Or a medium-sized town. Hell, there *were* towns around the country whose total populations were less than the number of people in his current family.

"Well, until recently," he began, "I grew up with six siblings and fourteen cousins."

"What happened recently?" She expected him to say something like that one of them had died, decreasing the numbers. She was definitely *not* expecting him to say what he did.

"Well, we found out that my late grandfather had

an older brother and that there were a whole bunch of Cavanaughs out there—protecting and serving," he quipped, "that we never knew about." He grinned at her as he approached the hotel. "As a matter of fact, we're still trying to get a handle on just how many more there are."

"There can't be *that* many."

Brennan just laughed in response. "Oh, but there can." He remembered the thought that had hit him when he arrived at that "welcome home" party for the former chief of the Aurora Police Department. "There's enough of us to form our own army if we wanted to."

"You're kidding, right?" When he didn't admit that she had him, Tiana looked at the man in the driver's seat more closely. He wasn't shifting in his seat or looking uncomfortable. "Right?" she pressed, beginning to think that maybe he actually *was* serious.

Brennan raised his broad shoulders in a casual shrug, then let them drop again. "If that's what you'd rather think, then okay, I'm kidding."

Obviously that was *not* the answer she was accepting because she realized that it wasn't true. "There's that many of you?" she finally asked. "The truth, now," she cautioned. "I want the truth."

"Uh-huh."

Brennan heard her sigh to herself. There was something almost wistful about the sound.

His hunch was confirmed when he heard her murmur, "It must be nice."

"Sometimes," he agreed. "But when you're growing

up, there're times when it really feels confining, like there's always someone watching you, making sure you don't screw up—even if you want to."

They got out of the sedan as Brennan gave the hotel valet the keys. "Something tells me that being watched wasn't exactly much of a concern for you."

She had his number, Brennan thought with a laugh. They walked through the hotel lobby to the bank of elevators.

"Let's just say I wasn't really trying to impress anyone with my angelic behavior."

Angelic was definitely not a word she would have used to describe the boy he had to have been. "Not even your mom?"

That made him think for a second. He pressed the button for the elevator. The doors opened immediately. "Well, I didn't want to cause her any grief, but on the other hand, I liked being me."

"Let me guess," Tiana said as they rode up to his floor. "You liked being wild and free, right?"

He half nodded, then corrected, "I prefer calling it independent. Sounds more adult," he explained.

She was trying to get a better understanding of the person she was working with. The person she was trusting with her sister's life, not to mention the small but very real fact that she was becoming increasingly more attracted to him. "How old were you at the time?"

"Ten."

Most ten-year-olds think an adult is something they want to avoid being at all costs. "Kind of young for an 'adult,'" she commented.

"I was an adult-in-training if you prefer," he quipped.

She laughed, shaking her head. "I really wish I'd known you back then."

His eyes met hers. There went her stomach again, she thought.

"Likewise," he told her.

His comment surprised her. "Why me?" she asked as they entered the suite.

Locking the door and putting the chain in place, Brennan turned to face her. "So that maybe I'd have a shot at keeping those frowns you're so prone to at bay. So that maybe I'd have a chance at hearing your laughter without having the sound come across as being so guarded."

She looked at Brennan, not knowing what to make of him. That he even noticed that about her was something she found surprising.

"And that's important?" she asked skeptically.

"Yes," he told her quietly, "that's important."

"Why?" she asked, wanting to be able to understand why he would feel that way.

Did he think of her as someone to be pitied? That had her back up, and yet she had a hard time actually believing that he would feel that way. He certainly didn't act as if he found her lacking, and there was nothing condescending about his manner toward her.

"Because I think you're capable of experiencing a great deal more happiness than you're allowing yourself to feel."

She sighed, shaking her head. She was a stranger to him, and anything he thought about her was just a guess on his part, nothing more. "You have no idea what I feel."

"No, but I'm willing to listen to you if you'll trust me enough to hear what you have to say."

"Stop it," she ordered. He was getting to her, making her feel as if she could open up to him, as if she could unburden herself, and she couldn't. He wasn't a regular, stable person in her life. He was just passing through. He'd be gone before she knew it. She *couldn't* act as if he was a fixture, because he wasn't. "You're being nice to me again."

"Is that what I'm doing?" he asked. Inclining his head, he said, "Sorry."

"No, you're not," she insisted.

"Busted," he replied, as both his eyes and his fingertips ever so lightly caressed her face.

Tiana pulled her head back—or thought she did. When she realized that she hadn't, she knew that she was about to go somewhere she had never been to before.

And that place was called Trouble.

Chapter 14

Less than a heartbeat later, Tiana was undoing him with her lips. Small, butterfly kisses along the side of his neck that were impossible to resist and were, in effect, driving him utterly crazy.

"We really should use this time to sleep, you know," he told her, though he wasn't doing anything to stop her.

She had no idea what had come over her. It was as if some invisible elastic band inside her had just snapped and everything that had been held so tightly together no longer was.

"I know," she murmured hoarsely, the words warm against his skin as she continued kissing him.

He should be holding her away at arms' length, but he just couldn't get himself to do it, no matter how much he knew he was supposed to be the one in control.

Still, he attempted to reason with her—or more accurately, with himself. "The human body only has so much energy. Once it's gone and it's not replenished, we might wind up falling down on the job."

His words of reason fell on deaf ears—*two* sets of deaf ears because he wasn't taking his own advice.

The more she kissed him, the more excited she became—especially when she heard his breathing become ever so slightly labored. The fact that she was having an effect on him was incredibly heady for her— she'd never been down this trail before.

"Can't do that," she agreed, paying strictly lip service to his display of common sense.

Unable to continue being merely the recipient, Brennan began tracing the same sort of trail along her neck and throat that she had initiated on his. "So we stop?"

She shivered as his breath literally created goose bumps along her skin.

"Yes. But in a minute," she qualified with effort. The words were not coming easily. "We stop in a minute." Tiana's mouth covered his—just for a second she promised herself. "Maybe two."

"Or five," he agreed, reclaiming her lips. The kiss went deeper than the ones before, leaving a promise of something more to come.

"Sounds like a plan," Tiana said with a heartfelt sigh that came from the bottom of her toes even as her adrenaline went into overdrive.

Brennan stopped feasting on the skin along her shoulders and throat and looked at her.

"Venus?"

Her head was swimming and she found it increasingly difficult to concentrate. "Hmm?"

"Stop talking."

She smiled into his eyes. "You, too."

"Deal," he whispered, his breath skimming along the skin just above her breasts.

And then there was no need for words, no place for them, either. They were completely blotted out by the deeds that followed.

Her pulse racing, Tiana felt as if she had to outrun her thoughts, the thoughts that told her that this was no time for something like this to be happening. That she needed to keep her mind focused, not utterly, hopelessly enthralled the way it was at this moment.

But her feelings were so hard to ignore, especially since she had finally given up all hope of *ever* feeling like this. She'd wanted to, tried to, then resigned herself to the fact that there was just something broken inside her. That because of her harsh upbringing, she was never going to even remotely *think* that she was in love or even some reasonable facsimile thereof.

She would never feel that wild rush that would make her throw caution to the winds just to become intimate with a man.

In pursuit of this precious sensation, she had pushed herself to the brink a couple of times, only to pull back and run before anything of consequence happened. For that, she'd been called a tease and worse, subjected to a volley of hurtful words and left to wonder what was wrong with her.

Why couldn't she feel what other women claimed to feel?

So she had come to the realization that the magic others claimed so vocally had entered their lives was never going to be part of hers. She'd given up and told herself it was okay, that she didn't care. She had her work and she had Janie and eventually, Janie would get married. Janie would have a family and she would share that with her sister, be happy for her sister.

It was enough.

She'd almost made herself believe that.

And then suddenly, here, with this man, she realized that someone else's happiness, even her beloved sister's happiness, wasn't going to be enough.

Wouldn't begin to really fill the emptiness inside her.

But this, here with Brennan, would satisfy the ache that she's always denied feeling. Or at least the satisfaction would be there for a little while. That was enough for now.

With that thought centermost in her mind, she gave herself up to the wild, thrilling feeling making its way throughout her entire being, revving up every single motor within her.

"Oh, baby, what is it? What is it?" Brennan asked, stunned at the sudden increase in pace and urgency of the way she was moving and making love with him.

One moment, they'd been teasing each other, grasping a little bit of happiness and salvation in a world filled with spirit-breaking burdens and responsibilities. The next, it seemed as if she had suddenly ratcheted up her pace, seeking to satisfy a suddenly unappeasable appetite.

Framing her face with his hands as he looked at her, Brennan asked, concerned, "What's wrong?"

"Nothing," she cried, pulling out of his hold and then feverishly kissing him as if she were afraid that the next moment, all this would just stop, vanishing into thin air.

"You're breaking the pact," Tiana accused. "You're talking."

Ordinarily, he'd just let himself enjoy what was happening, enjoy the sex, pure and simple. But he found himself more heavily invested than that with this woman, and what was happening went beyond a feverish frenzy of the blood.

Why?

Was she afraid they'd get a call in from Duncan and be forced to stop? He knew that was a possibility, but he also had a feeling that it might still be a while before Roland said or did anything that would make Duncan call them back to the hotel.

Something else was at the bottom of her behavior. But what?

"We can take this slow," he told her, catching her hands as Tiana was about to drag his shirt off his torso.

"We don't have time for slow," she said breathlessly, trying to pull her hands free of his grip.

It was tighter than she thought.

Still holding her hands, Brennan looked into her

eyes and said softly, "Yes, we do," his voice low, gentle, as if he was trying to gain the confidence of someone who had been abused.

Now that he thought about it, he realized that he had gotten those kinds of vibrations from her more than once before.

It made sense to him now.

Someone had hurt her, possibly damaged her, and she was trying to outdistance her fears before they closed in on her and prevented her from enjoying what could be a very beautiful thing between two people who had feelings for each other.

"Trust me, Tiana," Brennan assured her, "it's better slow."

She blinked, staring at him as his words registered. "That's the first time you've actually called me by my name," she pointed out, surprised.

A smile curved his mouth. "I was saving it for a special occasion," he told her, lightly brushing his lips against the side of her neck. "Like this one."

She melted, absolutely melted. Any possible hope she had of maintaining control completely dissolved.

Her eagerness, her desire to make love with him before something stopped her, was still there, but she let him set the pace, let him take the lead and show her exactly what it was that she had been missing all this time.

Brennan made love to her slowly, lyrically, with his hands, with his eyes and with his lips. They moved in concert from the front room with its sofa to the room behind it with its spacious queen-sized bed and comforter that whispered faintly of vanilla and lavender.

Her body heated quickly, her temperature rising another degree each time he kissed her, each time he touched her. Tiana could feel her body priming, wanting his.

Wanting him.

This time, as she increased her urgent pace, he was unable to keep her in check—mainly because he was having difficulty keeping *himself* in check.

This woman whom he found hard to read had tapped in to his control, his resistance. An area that was *not* subject to any of his usual restraints.

Brennan now experienced a heady and insatiable desire to make love with her, to become one with her. The more he tried to hold himself back, the greater the urgency to give her everything—all of his passion, all of his longing.

Naked and damp with sweat and desire, they tumbled onto the bed, touching, caressing, possessing, feeding their souls and draining any and all available energy, however little was still left.

Moving her beneath him, his hands joined with hers above her head, Brennan skimmed his lips along her throat, her face, her temples until he could no longer hold himself back. She had been moving so urgently beneath him, it was all he could do to restrain himself.

When he felt her raise her hips to his, the last of his resolve shattered.

Sealing his mouth to hers, he entered her.

But a heartbeat after Brennan began, he stopped, stunned.

Confused.

He began to draw his head back in order to look at her, but she took his edge away by pushing her hips up higher against his, not allowing him to pull back. Not allowing him to stop.

Brennan tasted her deep moan against his mouth and then felt her urgency return, taking him prisoner. They moved steadily together, going faster and faster until the pinnacle that he was familiar with and she so desperately desired to experience was finally reached.

It was worth it.

Worth the indecision, worth the pain and most of all, worth the risk of throwing all caution to the wind to feel something so indescribably wondrous that she had no words to frame what she had experienced.

The soft, comforting euphoria that wrapped itself around her held on tightly, and for one timeless moment, Tiana wished it would last forever. But the next moment, she was floating back to earth.

As her breathing grew less labored and returned to a more normal, steady cadence, she became aware of Brennan beside her.

Brennan holding her to him and looking at her.

The expression on his face was one of discomfort, for lack of a better term.

After a moment, Tiana put her own interpretation to his expression. She'd been expecting it.

And dreading it.

"You're disappointed," she concluded, wanting to

look away but forcing herself to look into his eyes. "I'm sorry I wasn't everything you hoped for."

"Disappointed?" he repeated. That wasn't the first word that came to his mind, but it would do, he supposed. "Yes, I'm disappointed. Disappointed you didn't tell me." Anger flared up in his chest. Anger at her—and mainly, anger at himself. It wasn't something he should have suspected, but once he'd become aware of it, he should have forced himself to stop, not wanted her so much that he continued what he'd been about. "Damn it, why didn't you tell me?" he demanded.

Tiana stared at the ceiling, willing herself not to cry. Tears gathered in her eyes, anyway. She struggled to keep them from falling.

"Couldn't find a way to work it into the conversation, I guess," she told him, her throat feeling raw, constricted as she spoke. "Maybe I should have had cards printed up. Tiana Drummond, career virgin." She took in a long breath and then let it out. "Except now I guess I'm not."

Brennan raised himself up on his elbow to look at her face. "It's not a joke."

"What do you want from me?" she cried, wishing she could just vanish. All the lovely sensations that had just been generated disappeared like so many soap bubbles scooped up by a strong wind. "You want me to apologize? Okay, I apologize."

"No, I don't want you to apologize," he shouted, not at her so much as at himself. "*I'm* the one who should be apologizing!"

Her mouth all but fell open as she stared at him,

his words echoing back in her head. "For what?" she demanded in utter confusion. "Unless I missed something, you didn't force yourself on me."

He drew a breath in, trying to calm himself. Shouting wasn't going to change anything, wasn't going to excuse his actions.

"No, but I might as well have. A woman's first time isn't supposed to be like this."

She continued to stare at him, at a complete loss. Could that actually be it? Could Brennan be apologizing because he hadn't wined and dined her, or whatever he thought the appropriate route to a first-time lovemaking encounter was supposed to be?

"I'm not complaining," Tiana said. Taking a breath, she raised herself up and at the same time, pushed him down onto the bed, pressing his back against the tangle of sheets. "Look, take this for whatever you think it's worth. Yes, this was my first time and it was everything, *everything* I could have hoped for. And more," she emphasized. "You were kind, gentle and you rocked my world. And if I, in some small way, returned the favor—or at least didn't bitterly disappoint you—then I think we can both walk away from what happened here without regrets. I know I have none."

Brennan still looked as if he wasn't convinced. "I didn't hurt you?"

Well, yes, there had been pain, but she'd been prepared for that. The rest of it had been a wondrous surprise—and well worth any pain that had been temporarily involved.

"Aren't you listening?" she asked him. As she

talked, she spread her hand out on his chest, gliding her fingertips slowly along the muscular ridges. "I have no regrets. And don't worry," she assured him in case he thought that in her mind, this meant that they were forever linked and she was looking to wear him down until he proposed. "I don't plan to follow you to the ends of the earth and bake you cookies—"

"No cookies?" he asked, sounding intentionally disappointed. "I like cookies."

His expression and tone made her laugh, evaporating the serious moment. "You are insane."

Brennan raised one eyebrow, as if questioning the fact that she even had to state the obvious. "Have you noticed my line of work?"

"Good point." Tiana leaned in and kissed him.

It was her intention to get up right after that, but Brennan cupped the back of her head and pulled her to him ever so slightly as he deepened the kiss that was supposed to be fleeting. She really *did* have every intention of getting up, but thirty seconds into the kiss and all desire to become vertical completely vanished.

A second wave of desire, higher, wider and more urgent than the first, washed over her. She forgot all about getting dressed, all about the hurt that had been generated when she thought he was disappointed that she was so inexperienced.

All she wanted was a second ride on the wild roller coaster that Brennan had wound up so artfully creating just for her.

This time the lovemaking started more languidly, more patiently, with a gentleness that almost brought tears to her eyes. But even so, the passion began to build until it was all but sending shock waves through her body, urging her to even greater heights, heights that, as inconceivable as it seemed to her, hadn't been attained last time.

What it showed her was that no matter how wondrous and awesome her initial experience had been, better was possible. And he was *the best*.

The climax, such an unexpected surprise the first time, now vibrated through Tiana not once, not twice, but a total of several times. They were all different, yet all equally earth-shaking in magnitude.

Tiana was a very willing student and she learned exceptionally fast.

It wasn't long before she surprised him, and at times during their second time around, Brennan found their roles reversed. Instinctive reactions had her being the teacher, turning him into the eager student.

She brought out things within him he hadn't thought were there. In addition, he felt a sense of bonding with her that heretofore had eluded him during his adult life.

This wasn't a woman of the moment, Brennan realized. Tiana was a woman he seriously wanted to return to at the end of the day.

Return to time and again.

Was this what a desire for commitment actually felt like?

Brennan didn't know. He had always assumed that a wife and kids—a family—were in his future. But that was for "someday" when he had done everything else he wanted to do. Maybe when he found another passion to dedicate himself to outside of law enforcement.

But now he wasn't so sure.

Now he began to think, as he gathered Tiana closer just to feel her heart beating against his, that maybe "someday" was a great deal closer than he had initially thought.

Maybe "someday" was actually here.

Chapter 15

Living strictly within the moment and effectively managing to exclude any dark, outside thoughts that would only undermine the way he felt right now, Brennan lightly brushed his lips against the top of her head. The scent of Tiana's hair made him think of an endless spring morning.

He savored the peaceful image, willing it to linger for a while.

"You know," he told her, "I rarely take second helpings and I've never gone for thirds."

Today was a day for firsts, he thought. And that included the way he responded to everything about this woman.

Tiana raised her head ever so slightly, her hair seductively slipping along his bare skin, enticing a man who was more than halfway there to begin with. She looked at him a little uncertainly.

"Are you saying what I think you're saying?" Tiana asked in amazement.

He played with a wisp of her hair at the nape of her neck, wrapping the red strand around his index finger. "I am," he told her.

She didn't frown so much as look a tad puzzled. "I know this makes me sound really naive, but..." She hesitated for a second before asking, "Is that normal?"

He grinned, amused. Her innocence warmed him. "For me or in general?"

Her shoulders moved in a puzzled shrug. "Whichever you feel most comfortable answering."

He did what he could to attempt to look serious. He succeeded only marginally. "No—and possibly."

Her mind did a double take. "What?"

He laughed, elaborating. "For me, no, I'm not generally—for lack of a better term—a repeater. Or at least I wasn't," he amended in light of what had just transpired today. "And I've never taken a poll among my friends, but I figure there've gotta be guys who don't get their fill, who're more or less insatiable. Those I think fall into the addict category. How interested are you in what's behind door number two?" he asked, referring to the second category.

"Not at all," she told him, shifting her body so that her upper torso was lying across his. "Door number one gets my vote all the way."

"Good to know," he murmured.

She lowered her mouth to his.

But just as they began to immerse themselves in each other again, giving lie to his statement about his limited repeat performance, Brennan's cell phone rang insistently.

Instantly alert, they shifted gears immediately, leaving their private personas behind and morphing back into police detectives, first and foremost.

"Cavanaugh," Brennan said the second he put the cell phone to his ear.

"I know your last name, bro."

Duncan was on the other end, just as he had assumed. He'd said his name automatically—and on the outside chance that it was someone else calling with information.

Brennan's body remained alert, ready. "What have you got?"

"You mean other than a numb butt?" his brother cracked. "Our boy just got a message that his presence is requested within the hour. I'm taking that to mean he might be meeting with someone who had the authority to order him around. In any case," Duncan pointed out, "that means he's going to be mobile."

As he listened to Duncan, Brennan looked around for his clothes. Spotting them on the floor, he pulled his pants over. He had no idea where his underwear was. For now, he'd skip getting a pair. He needed to be ready to go within seconds if his quarry was going to be on the move soon.

"If he leaves early, follow him," Brennan instructed, tucking the cell phone against his ear with his shoulder as he pulled on his trousers. "And have Valri call me with updates until you get to wherever it is that Roland is supposed to be going."

"You *do* realize that Valri and I are both off duty, right?" Duncan asked.

"Think of it as doing a good deed," Brennan told him. Out of the corner of his eye, he saw Tiana looking at him, obviously dying to ask questions but not wanting to interrupt in the event something crucial was being relayed. "If we can bring down this pervert's network, a lot of girls will be sleeping in their own beds soon. And a lot more will never know the utter terror of being abducted."

"You always did fight dirty," Duncan responded with a sigh.

Brennan laughed at his brother's complaint. "There's another way?"

"I guess you've got a point there, bro," Duncan relented.

"One more thing. If you do wind up having to follow him, remember to stay off his radar," Brennan warned. Neither Duncan nor Valri had been on the job as long as he had and neither one of them had ever needed to go undercover. He tended to be overprotective of his younger siblings.

"And here I was, all set to ram him at the first red light we come to," Duncan lamented. His voice grew serious as he reassured his brother, "Not my first rodeo, big brother."

"If this *was* about busting broncos, I wouldn't be half this concerned about the two of you," Brennan told him.

"Nice to know you care," Duncan replied dryly. "Mom would have been proud that her lectures to you actually took."

"Call me," Brennan ordered, not wanting to go in the direction his brother was heading. Duncan had a way of going on extended tangents. "And stay safe. Both of you," he added.

"Does this mean I can't push Valri in front of a truck? Ow!"

Brennan guessed that the unexpected exclamation of pain meant that Valri had punched Duncan's arm in retaliation for the crack. "Not today."

"Got it," Duncan replied dutifully.

The call was terminated on both ends.

Turning around, Brennan saw that Tiana was already dressed and ready to go. "Guess you filled in the blanks," he speculated, reaching for his shirt.

"You forgot your underwear," she pointed out, indicating the item that was on the floor on the far end of room.

Well, he wasn't about to stop to put them on now. That would entail getting undressed again.

"Gives me a head start on next time," Brennan told her with a wink.

"Next time?" she repeated. From the sound of it, they had a long afternoon and evening ahead of them. Was he actually thinking beyond the day?

Brennan nodded as he crossed to where his gun and holster were. "You know, like the time after 'this' time," he prompted. Checking to see that there was a bullet in each chamber of his weapon, he glanced in her direction. "Is that all right with you?"

Tiana grinned at him. She knew it wasn't very sophisticated or worldly of her, but she really didn't care. Once they accomplished this mission, she intended to enjoy the *hell* out of being with this man for as long as it lasted. She had no illusions about the situation, but she wasn't about to allow that to dampen a single iota of the relationship while it was in full swing.

"That's terrific with me," she assured him.

"Good." Doing a mental inventory of all the points he needed to cover to make sure he hadn't neglected something or left it to chance—mistakes cost lives— he was satisfied he hadn't forgotten anything or overlooked it. "Okay, let's go, then."

"Exactly where are we going?" she asked as she fell into step beside him.

"Back to where we left my car if Duncan doesn't call," he told her. "Wherever he tells us to go if it turns out that he's on the move."

Tiana was already on her way to the elevator. "Sounds good to me."

Duncan still hadn't called by the time Brennan and Tiana arrived in the general vicinity where he'd left his vehicle parked with his siblings in it.

Parking farther down the street than they'd initially been—thanks to an increase in traffic—they got out of the car quickly and made their way toward his sedan.

The moment they arrived, Duncan and Valri all but jumped out of the car.

"God, I've forgotten how boring everyone always said stakeouts were," Valri confided to her older brother and the woman who had apparently been in Brennan's company the whole time. Valri was dying to ask the latter a few questions, but now wasn't the time and she knew Brennan wouldn't appreciate her being so inquisitive—or nosy as he called it.

"He still holed up in the suite?" Brennan asked, nodding in the hotel's direction.

"According to the monitor, he hasn't moved a muscle. You ask me, I think he's pulling this 'slow' act because he's trying to get back at whoever's in charge for some reason."

"Get back at him for what?" Tiana asked. That sounded awfully petty to her, considering what was at stake here.

"Over some imagined slight or put-down he probably thought he'd received. This Roland character's pretty thin-skinned, if you ask me," Duncan told her.

"You got all that in the last hour?" Brennan asked rather skeptically. Maybe Duncan was evolving into a really decent detective after all, he mused, a feeling of pride slipping through him.

"More like two hours, and why so surprised?" Duncan asked. "You think you're the only clever one in the family who can make deductions?"

"The thought did cross my mind," Brennan deadpanned. "Okay, we'll take it from here," he told his brother and sister.

"It's all yours, bro," Duncan said, gesturing toward the monitor in the car. "See you this Sunday?"

From his tone, Duncan sounded as if asking was a mere formality. Since his brother had saved Andrew's life, Sunday dinners had become more or less a staple within their family—just as it had been and continued to be for the main branch of the family.

However, Brennan wasn't about to be hemmed in by tradition. "Not sure if I can make it. We might still be sitting here."

"From what I hear," Valri interjected, "Andrew Cavanaugh isn't a man who accepts excuses readily."

Brennan was in a position to know otherwise. "When you save a guy's life, you get a little leeway accorded to you," he confided, holding out Duncan's car keys.

"Gotta remember that the next time I save someone's life," Duncan replied as he took back his car keys. "Where—"

"Down the block, about halfway to the corner," Brennan told him, anticipating the rest of the question.

With a nod, Duncan and Valri went to find his sedan.

"You think your brother's right about Roland?" Tiana asked after Duncan and Valri had gone. "Or do you think that maybe Roland's onto us and said what he did just to toy with us?" she asked, coming back to the possibility she'd raised earlier.

"I still don't think Roland's bright enough to plant red herrings—he'd have to have someone pretending to be whoever was in charge call him on his cell for us to hear—and that presupposes that he's onto the fact that you planted a monitoring device on his person.

Acting isn't his forte. All he's good for is throwing his weight round and behaving as if he was important."

"Maybe 'Mr. Big,' whoever he is, got paranoid and called off the meeting," she guessed. Why else was Roland still inside the suite?

"Dealing with Roland, I'd be paranoid, too. Should things start going south, there's no question that Roland will do whatever it takes to keep himself out of going to prison."

However, Tiana wasn't as sure as he was. "If Roland turns state's evidence, he'll be looking over his shoulder the rest of his life."

"At least he'll have a shoulder to look over," Brennan reminded her. "Considering that there have been a number of dead girls found in most of the cities this traveling sex circus has been through, the death penalty is on that same table," Brennan said. "'Singing' for us is actually the better way to go for middle men like Roland. Our job will be to convince him of that."

"Something tells me that might not be too difficult to do. One look at his future cell mates in the general population and that man will sing soprano before you can request the aria from *Carmen*."

"You know opera?" he asked, surprised at the mention of the classical play.

"I go to the occasional performance when it doesn't interfere with my work. I suppose you think that's hopelessly uncool in your world," she wondered out loud.

"I don't know about 'cool' and 'uncool,' but my mother liked operas. The thought of having to sit through one would make Dad cringe, so she used to take me instead. I always told her I thought it was all a bunch of noise in a language I couldn't understand, but to be honest, there were some I liked, especially after she explained the stories to me."

Tiana understood him better than he thought. "You just couldn't admit you liked them because you'd be made fun of by the other kids."

Brennan inclined his head. "Something like that, maybe," he admitted with a shrug. "Funny how much the opinion of others means when you're that age."

It wasn't always confined to just a narrow range of age. "Any age, depending on the person." The memory was painful—but it only became more so if she allowed it to remain inside her and fester. "Janie thought the sun rose and set around Wayne."

"Wayne," Brennan repeated, momentarily drawing a blank. And then he remembered. "That would be—"

She nodded, anticipating his response. "The dead guy in the motel."

"Ah." He'd been right, he thought.

Part of her wished she had found a way to keep Janie at home. She would have been safe then. But she knew it would have been wrong to rob her sister of her independence, or stifle it. There had to be a happy medium. But she would explore this *after* she found her sister.

"When I told her to be careful around Wayne, that he might not have her best interests at heart, she told me that I was just jealous because she preferred Wayne over me."

"You turned out to be right. The guy didn't have her best interests at heart—just his own," Brennan pointed out.

Tiana sighed. "Somehow being right is small comfort if I can't find Janie before that scum pulls up stakes and sneaks out of the country."

He kept one eye on the monitor as he went on talking. "Hey." He reached over and squeezed her hand. "I promised you we'd find her in time, and we will. I don't go back on my word."

"You really can't guarantee something like that," she reminded him. Tension, fed by fear, crackled in her voice. "You're not God."

"Well, that's a blow to my ego," he cracked drolly. "And here I thought that you—"

Brennan stopped talking abruptly when something on the monitor caught his eye. Roland was taking a cell phone out of his pocket and talking on it. From his movements, it had rung and caught him off guard. Though he looked very animated while speaking, not a word was heard inside the car.

There was no audio.

"We've lost the sound," Brennan realized in frustration. He slanted a glance in her direction. "You wouldn't happen to read lips, would you?"

"I can if I can see them," she told him, frustrated, "but this monitor is just too small. Besides, even if I could, we still can't hear whoever's on the cell."

He figured that had to be the man in charge—or whoever that person had authorized to call in his stead. "Well, whoever it is has Mister Not-So-Big jumping to attention." They might have lost the sound, but they still had video. "Now he's calling over one of his oversized bodyguards. No, wait, he's calling over both of them. Looks like there's going to be a road trip in their near future," he speculated.

She closed her eyes, feeling incredibly grateful. It looked as if they were *finally* getting somewhere. "And we have liftoff."

A crackling noise came on, then faded and returned, doing this intermittently as the audio struggled to make a resurrection. But at the moment, there was no real need for it to be working. The micro device that Tiana had planted on Roland's person showed that he was on his way out of his suite. He was following one bodyguard, and the other was clearly behind him, obviously watching the man's back.

"The curtain is finally going up on what could be the third act," Brennan said to her, turning on the car's ignition.

"Do you think he's going to where the girls are being kept?" Tiana asked him nervously.

Brennan knew what he'd be going through if he were trying to rescue one of his sisters. He completely sympathized with Tiana.

"All we can do is follow him and find out." Spotting the car as it emerged from the hotel's parking structure, Brennan began to tail the vehicle at a safe distance. "Call Duncan and tell him we're on the move."

She had her cell phone out in a second. But then she stopped. "I don't—"

"Sorry. I forgot." He rattled off his brother's cell phone number for her.

She hit each number on the keypad as quickly as he recited it. She heard the phone ringing on the other end. Someone picked up on the fourth ring.

"Cavanaugh."

"Duncan?"

There was a moment's hesitation before he answered, "Yes, who's this?"

"Put it on speaker," Brennan told her. When she did, he directed his words to his brother on the other end of the call. "The fox has just left his lair and appears to be on his way to the henhouse."

"Ah, Brennan. Of course," his brother said wearily. "Exactly why did you call? You want me to applaud?"

"Save it until I've done something applause-worthy." He made a left at the light after watching the vehicle Roland was in execute the same turn. "At the moment, I want you to be my backup."

"You do remember that you have other brothers you could call, right?" Duncan asked.

Brennan grinned. "I remember—but you take orders so well."

"Yeah, well, I've gotta go—"

Not one to give up, Brennan raised his voice. "And I have two courtside seats to the next Lakers game for you and the basketball fan of your choice."

That stopped Duncan from hanging up. "You think you can bribe me?"

Brennan laughed. "I know I can. Don't pretend otherwise. When it comes to your obsession with basketball, you're not exactly clearheaded. Don't forget, I've known you since you were born."

"Okay." Duncan sighed, resigned. "Tell me your twenty and I'll be your backup."

"You've renewed my faith in the power of bribery." With a grin, Brennan slanted a look toward Tiana. "That's your cue, Venus," he told her. "Fill him in on the route we're taking."

She was quick to comply.

Chapter 16

Pursuit of Roland's black sedan had all but ground to a halt. Literally. Following the vehicle at a safe distance, they found themselves driving into a very upscale area whose well-kept-up streets were far too narrow to accommodate any sort of standard flow of traffic.

"This is more like a drip, not a flow, if you ask me," Tiana commented impatiently. Since she was unfamiliar with the area, she turned to Brennan and asked, "Exactly where are we?"

He was surprised she didn't know, but he kept that to himself. "Right now we're inching our way through Rodeo Drive."

She knew the name. So this was what it looked like, she thought, focusing on the boutique windows that faced the street. There was a profusion of expensive clothing, accessories and jewelry as far as the eye could see. All of it left her cold. She viewed it as just so much avarice. In her opinion, there were far better, more worthwhile things to spend money on than a thousand-dollar pair of stilettos.

"This is the place with all the fancy, pricey stores, right?" she asked him.

It tickled him that Tiana didn't sound as if she would have enjoyed having a shopping spree here. "The very same."

"Well, I really doubt that Roland's got Christmas shopping in mind," she said, exasperated. "Why is he doing this?"

"Maybe to *look* as if he was on the way to do some expensive gift buying and throw off anyone who might be tailing him." Coming to yet another stop—he'd lost track of how many that made—Brennan glanced at his watch. "Being stuck in this kind of gridlock for any amount of time is enough to fray a saint's patience."

Her mouth curved despite the gravity of the situation, recalling the way things had been a couple of hours ago. "And you are definitely not a saint."

Brennan laughed, fairly certain that his mind was homing in on the same thought she was having. "Not the last time I checked."

"So, we're not turning around, are we?" she asked, her mind scrambling for a way to convince him to continue in case he answered yes.

"It's just as gridlocked behind us as it is in front of us. It's got to let up sometime. And we might as well see if he really *is* shopping or just up to something," he said with a hint of resignation.

"That gets my vote," she said. "Maybe he's smarter than we gave him credit for."

"Maybe. Or maybe he's just following instructions that we didn't get to hear because the audio went down," he theorized.

A light blue van darted out from the left, nearly cutting them off had he not stepped on the gas and swerved to circumvent the vehicle. A collision was ever so narrowly avoided by inches. He'd expected Tiana to scream or rattle off terrified instructions after the fact. But all she had done was suck in her breath. The woman had nerves of steel, he thought with no small admiration.

Once clear of the van, he spared her a fleeting glance. "Well, one good thing. At least I know you're not a front-seat driver."

"You wouldn't listen to anything I said, anyway," she pointed out. "Besides, I figure you have more experience driving these streets than I do."

"That I do," he agreed, although not exactly happily. Driving here at any time of the day was a challenge he would have rather done without.

They were back to crawling and he saw the black sedan he was following. It was three car lengths ahead of them but still very visible.

For now.

He glanced at Tiana for a beat longer and took note of the imprints in the armrest that was closest between them. She'd dug her nails in. Hard. He found that rather comforting.

"Apparently, not all of you trusts my driving as much as you think."

She noted where he was looking. Her nails had gone in deeply enough to not only leave marks, but to tear away some of the leather.

"Sorry," she apologized, "that's just an automatic reaction. I was bracing for what looked like it was going to be a huge collision." She flashed him a smile. "Thanks for not having one."

"That would seriously impede having this come to a happy ending," he commented, his eyes back on the road and watching Roland's sedan intently. "And I promised you a happy ending."

Though she knew in her heart of hearts that there was no way Brennan could actually guarantee that, she still clung to his words. Maybe if she believed hard enough, it would come to pass.

"That you did," Tiana murmured under her breath.

Brennan still managed to hear her. "And like I told you, I always keep my word," he told her. He grew serious for just a moment. "I don't intend to change my pattern now."

"Okay." Tiana was doing her best to sound nonchalant and together, but the very real tension she felt building up inside her was enough to blow her apart if she let it.

So she wouldn't let it, Tiana told herself fiercely. She had to hold it together until they found Janie. It didn't matter what happened to her after that, but she *had* to get Janie out of this horrible situation. She refused to entertain the possibility of any other sort of scenario coming to pass.

Close to forty-five minutes later, they were finally clear of the small, packed shopping area and on their way at something approaching a normal speed.

"I've never seen so many Bentleys and Ferraris in my life," she told Brennan.

As with the merchandise on display on Rodeo Drive, to Tiana, paying the kind of money that one of those automobiles had to cost was a terrible waste of money, money that could be better spent elsewhere, on causes that made a difference.

"Have you figured out where we're going yet?" she asked.

Considering the direction the vehicle transporting Roland was going in, Brennan figured he had a pretty good idea about the man's destination's end. "I think he's headed for Brentwood."

That sounded vaguely familiar, although she wasn't really sure what context she'd heard it in. "Is that like Beverly Hills?"

"Very much so," he said, just managing to squeak through a light. "Pricier for the most part."

She tried to reconcile the thought that people who spent so much time and effort on the outer trappings of success would be involved in something like sex trafficking. "You think the girls are being kept somewhere around there?"

"If they are, the accommodations are going to be a great deal better than a run-down motel or an empty warehouse." Both of which had been considered possibilities when the investigation got under way. In Brentwood there were large regal homes—mansions, really—dotting the hillsides. "I couldn't afford this. Neither could anyone I know."

As far as she could see, there seemed to be only one reason Roland would be traveling in this area. "Maybe he's going to meet with whoever's in charge."

"That would be my guess." For a second, he focused on something other than his target. "You see Duncan anywhere around?"

Tiana twisted around in her seat, but from this vantage point, she was unable to locate his brother's vehicle.

"No," she answered, at which point she took out her cell phone and hit Redial on the keypad.

"Cavanaugh," Duncan bit off, answering on the third ring. "Is this a wild-goose chase?" he asked, obviously assuming that it was his brother calling. It was hard to miss the impatience in his voice.

Brennan spared Tiana a smile. He liked the fact that she'd anticipated his next request and had gotten Duncan on the phone without being asked.

"If it is," he told Duncan, "I've got my eye on the goose that's leading this parade. He's still three cars ahead of us, but I've got him in my sights. Where are you?" Brennan asked.

"Lost amid the rich and famous." Duncan gave him the name of a street.

Duncan wasn't all that far behind him, Brennan thought. He told his brother the street he was currently on and gave him a description of the surrounding area to facilitate matters.

"I think our quarry is going to a house in Brentwood. Presumably for a meeting."

"I sure as hell hope so after all this trouble," Duncan grumbled. "You know how I feel about traffic."

"Never met anyone who was crazy about it," Brennan said. "I'll call you when I get to wherever it is I'm going."

The lots the custom-made houses in this particular neighborhood were on were huge in comparison to the rest of the homes in this region of Southern California. They were coming upon a stately mansion normally secured behind tall black gates that rendered it inaccessible to the rest of the world.

But at the moment, the gates were standing wideopen. A parade of hugely upscale automobiles were winding their way through the gates, including the black sedan they were following. The cars all appeared to be headed toward a large, imposing-looking, multicolumned mansion in the distance.

Clusters of expensive cars were parked everywhere, with valets hurrying to and fro between them.

Tiana sat up a little straighter, taking everything in at once. "I think it looks like we're going to be crashing a party."

"Not with that kind of security on duty," Brennan pointed out, indicating the men stopping each vehicle as it came within yards of the house. "Those guys are far too menacing-looking to be valets."

Tiana suddenly had an idea. "Pull over to the side," she instructed.

"Why?" Brennan asked, following the single-word question with another one. "Where?"

"There, go to the extreme rear," she said, pointing out where she wanted him to turn. "Where the delivery trucks are."

She definitely sounded as if she had a plan. They worked well together, he couldn't help thinking. Brennan drove to exactly where Tiana had pointed. "What do you have in mind?"

"Well, we can't crash the party as guests," she reasoned. "But nobody really ever notices the help at one of these functions."

"We'll need uniforms if we're going to try to blend in," he pointed out.

She'd already thought of that. "We either bribe two people who are approximately our size—or knock them out and tie them up, whichever way you think works best."

Brennan laughed, turning the headlights of his vehicle off as he snaked his way around the rear of the mansion. He was heading for a row of mature Leyland Cypresses.

"Roland might or might not be smarter than he looks, but you are definitely more devious than you look," he told Tiana. There was appreciation as well as admiration in his voice.

His comment warmed her.

They left his sedan parked behind the Leyland Cypresses. The trees, which resembled large Christmas trees, looked like tall, dark green sentries and hid the car well.

The moment they were parked and he cut off the motor, Brennan called Duncan as he'd arranged earlier. He filled his brother in as to where they were by providing the address—and told him to wait for his call before coming onto the property.

"What are you going to be doing in the meantime, 'partying'?" Duncan asked, only half kidding.

Brennan would if he could, but that wasn't an option. He and Tiana needed to move around unnoticed. "You know that oath we all took to protect and serve? Well, we'll be doing the serving part," Brennan told him just before terminating the call. He knew he'd fired up Duncan's curiosity and he got a kick out of that.

Within a couple of minutes, he and Tiana were inching their way closer to the rear of the house and the three large trucks that were the center of the activity here. Brennan played it by ear.

In the end, he decided it was easier to do it both ways.

With Tiana's help he knocked out two food servers, a man and a woman whose sizes approximated theirs. The uniforms they were wearing were stripped off. Unconscious, the duo offered no resistance. The couple were subsequently bound and gagged and left in their underwear.

The servers were then deposited in the trunk of Brennan's sedan, but not before several large bills were tucked away on their person, payment for their "cooperation," as unwilling and unintentional as that service might have been.

The trunk locked, Brennan and she made their way back to the hub of all the activity. All types of food and liquid libation, not to mention everything that went with the serving of that food, made its appearance in the vicinity and was then taken inside.

"Good fit," Brennan commented as he looked Tiana over just before they merged with the ebb and flow of all the activity. "Now what?"

She looked at him, clearly surprised that he was asking her. "Hey, it's your plan. You call the shots."

"Now we grab something to carry inside and blend in as we look around. I've got a feeling that the main entertainment isn't going to be a showing of the newly restored *The Wizard of Oz*."

"You, too, huh?" As they approached the truck closest to them, Brennan caught her hand. Stopping in her tracks, she looked at him, waiting. "Just remember, if we get separated, no heroics. Get back to the car as fast as possible."

"Is that what you plan to do?" she asked. She didn't want to be treated with kid gloves. This was *her* sister they were looking to rescue. Yes, there were other girls and they would be saved, as well, but it was the hunt for Janie that had brought both of them to this juncture.

"I said if 'we' get separated," Brennan pointed out.

He was being evasive, she thought. He knew how to use words effectively—but he couldn't fool her. "You're not really answering my question, you know," Tiana told him.

"Showtime," he suddenly announced with lips that were hardly moving.

He would have made a great ventriloquist, she thought. He was also good at avoiding answering questions directly.

"Hey, you two, get your butts out here and hustle." The order was barked by a less-than-friendly-looking bald man who gave the impression that he felt any time he spent out here with the "help" was really beneath him. "Do whatever else you want on your own time. I'm not paying you good money to be all over each other," the sharp-featured man snapped, scowling. He gestured angrily toward a workstation that had been set up. "Those wine goblets aren't going to fill and circulate themselves," he stressed, barking out orders.

"Yes, sir." Tiana all but saluted, snapping to it cheerfully. She gave the man an appropriately meek, subservient smile as she hurried in through the back entrance.

She and Brennan headed toward the table that had at least a dozen empty glasses arranged on it. They each picked up a bottle of wine from a nearby case and began to fill the goblets, which they then placed on round, gold-leaf-embossed serving trays.

It wasn't long before another straw boss with dictator delusions separated them, taking possession of Brennan.

"I need somebody with a strong back," the heavyset man told Brennan, the buttons on his white tux shirt straining valiantly against their holes with each breath he took. "We've got tables to set up in the back," he said condescendingly.

Tiana was on her own—and fairly certain that Brennan's previous warning regarding separation hadn't been intended to describe this sort of situation. They had just gotten here, and she for one wasn't leaving until she was sure this was just a harmless party and not an orgy using helpless young girls as unwilling participants.

Tiana carried trays of wine goblets for the next half hour, winding her way through groups of people, most of whom, as she'd hoped, didn't notice her at all. However, she did catch a few staring unabashedly at her as if she were some exotic meal and they hadn't eaten in months.

The leers she saw aimed in her direction had her promising herself a very long, very hot bath once this was finally over. God knew she could use it.

During that time, as she collected empty goblets and offered filled ones in their place, she also noticed that about 80 percent of the guests were males. The women attending the party were few, mostly seeming like window dressing rather than equals to the men they were with.

A couple of times, she saw Brennan from across the room. Each time the man who had commandeered Brennan had him doing something that required brute strength.

It was becoming more and more apparent to Tiana that this party had been thrown together hastily, for what purpose was yet unclear. It did seem that no money was spared, but despite that, it looked as if things were not progressing as smoothly as they might have, although she suspected that none of the guests noticed.

One guest almost walked right into her as he tried to ambush an older man who was standing several feet behind her.

"Hey, Wilson," the man called out to his quarry. "How much longer do we have to wait?"

"Patience, Mr. Walker, patience. Everything comes to him who waits," the man behind her advised.

The man called Walker looked less than patient. "Yeah, well, it feels like we've been waiting around forever."

"Soon," the man replied in an incredibly soothing voice. "Soon." The voice also sounded vaguely familiar to her, but that familiarity was currently filtering down to her through a fog.

Where had she heard it before? And exactly in what context?

As she half turned, pretending to offer the man behind her the last glass of wine on her tray, her heart all but stopped.

She recognized him immediately.

Chapter 17

Wilson Ashcroft.

Stunned, Tiana almost said his name out loud. She had never seen the man up close, or even in person, but she had seen his photograph on a number of occasions in the newspaper, as well as in an extensive national magazine interview about six months ago.

Ashcroft was considered one of the wealthiest men in the country. In general, it was noted that he liked keeping a low profile but was the go-to person when it came to underwriting fund-raisers as well as generously giving donations to almost every large organized charity in existence.

And there were also rumors—well-researched rumors—that he had been instrumental in getting more than one political candidate elected, both on the state level and on the national one. More than one grateful political official owed his or her career to Ashcroft's efforts and generosity.

What was a man like that doing being involved in something so heinous as the wanton sex trafficking of any individuals, much less underage girls?

There *had* to be some mistake, yet there he was, less than three feet away from her, talking to a man who looked as if he were once removed from a Neanderthal in a tailored suit.

Appearances could be deceiving. Maybe Ashcroft and Neanderthal Man were talking about something else, something as inconsequential as what was being served for the buffet dinner. She reminded herself that so far she hadn't seen any evidence of there being anything wrong. The only element that seemed out of sync was that Roland was here. She'd seen him milling around several of the guests earlier.

But then, for all she and Brennan knew, maybe this was just some social commitment on Roland's part. She was fairly certain that when a man of Ashcroft's stature said, "Come," someone as socially conscious as Roland would all but break his neck to do just that.

Ashcroft, of average height and medium, somewhat unimpressive build, still managed to stand out in a crowd. It was his demeanor and his manner that set him apart from the average man. Aside from his vast fortune, a fortune he had amassed on his own rather than just inheriting, Ashcroft was a man that made others stop talking and take notice of him.

More than that, to *listen* to him. He took center

stage whenever he opened his mouth. Wilson Ashcroft had a quality about him that belonged exclusively to leaders. It was more than just his piercing blue eyes, his thick mane of silver hair or his chiseled profile. It was something inherent that rose to the surface the moment he began to speak. The cadence was low, almost soothing, but it left the listener caught up in whatever subject Ashcroft raised.

Crossing to her, Ashcroft plucked a goblet of red wine from her tray, smiled at her and nodded. "Thank you, my dear."

Since she'd arrived and donned this uniform, no one had even acknowledged that she was there or had rendered a service. That was apparently taken for granted since she was supposedly being paid for it. This gathering was obviously at Ashcroft's behest and yet he treated her with respect and had just now acted as if he and she were equals in every sense of the word, rather than billionaire and servant.

Charisma, she realized. The man had it in spades and was utilizing it effortlessly—and well.

"And one for my friend here," Ashcroft requested of her, nodding at the man whom he had referred to as "Mr. Walker."

"Don't try to dull my senses, Wilson. You know what I want." Walker took the goblet nonetheless and absently sipped from it.

"Yes, I do," Ashcroft acknowledged, lowering his voice although still keeping it pleasant. "However, if you don't get hold of yourself, Mr. Walker, I'll be forced to have one of my security people escort you from the premises to your vehicle and send you on your way." He looked directly into his guest's eyes. "Have I made myself clear?"

The smile never left Ashcroft's lips as he spoke, but Tiana felt a cold chill zip up and down her spine, all but freezing it.

Tiana did her best to look as if she hadn't heard any of the conversation. Instead, keeping her eyes forward, she continued weaving her way through the ever-growing gathering of guests.

Though she kept focused on her task and oblivious to specific people, Tiana did manage to covertly keep an eye on the party's host. Beneath hooded eyes she watched as Ashcroft worked the crowd, pausing to speak to one person here, another there, appearing to touch base with as many of the attendees as possible.

Everyone, apparently, wanted to exchange a few words with the man and to bask, if possible, for a moment or two in his aura. The general supposition was that if he so chose to smile upon them, wonderful things might befall the recipient of the great man's attention.

Every so often, she would see Ashcroft being approached by someone he'd waved over. A thin, almost nondescript man in a suit who was obviously on his staff rather than an attendee at the party. Ashcroft and his employee would exchange a few words, or rather, Ashcroft would say something and the man, who she judged was in his mid-forties, would nod and then make his way to one of the guests, taking him from the large room and bringing him, she assumed, to another part of the mansion.

Tiana watched this odd chain of events happen twice, then waited for the next time because she was determined that this time, she would follow the duo when they left the room.

She was studying the scene so intently, she nearly jumped when she felt someone lightly touch her on the shoulder.

To her relief, she found herself looking up into Brennan's eyes.

"Anything?" he asked her in a low whisper. Placing his tray down on the table in front of her, he began to arrange fresh goblets and pour wine into them.

Tiana followed suit. She'd filled two goblets before she told him, "I think the man behind all this is Wilson Ashcroft."

Brennan, who for the most part had been in another area of the mansion entirely, allowed a note of surprise to register in his voice. He hadn't seen this coming. "The philanthropist?"

"It's his house and seems to be his event," she told Brennan. "Every so often, he has one of his security people take one of the guests off to some other area. Could be that's where they're keeping the girls—the live part of the entertainment for a selected few," she bit off sarcastically.

He turned from his refilled tray and looked at her for a moment. Ashcroft was supposed to be one of the good guys. "Doesn't sound plausible."

She gave him something to chew on. All too often,

well-known people—especially those with money—
didn't think that the rules applied to them.

"Maybe he thinks he's put too many people in the
right offices to worry about getting caught—or even
to consider that what he was involved in was wrong."

Was Janie here somewhere in this overly large collection of rooms? Was she being hurt—or worse—
while she stood here, undecided and vacillating as to
her next move?

"You've got a point," Brennan acknowledged, raising his tray up. It was time to return to his area and
continue serving people who looked right through him.
But before he left Tiana's company, he warned, "Don't
do anything stupid without me."

She deliberately flashed a quick smile in his direction. "I'll give you a quick call when I feel like doing
something stupid," she promised.

All sorts of alarms went off in Brennan's head. He
knew he was going to have to keep tabs on Tiana as
well as locating Ashcroft. That might be a bit more
difficult than it had sounded, but something in his gut
told him that he couldn't trust Tiana not to get it into
her head that she was just as bulletproof as the person she was after.

Almost twenty minutes passed before she saw Ashcroft sending off his security man to take charge of
another one of his guests, separating him from the
other party attendees.

As before she saw that no words were exchanged
with the guest, but the moment Ashcroft's security

man walked past him, the man Ashcroft had previously been talking with, a man who had, judging from the thickness of the white envelope, just handed Ashcroft a sizable donation, fell into step behind him.

As unobtrusively as possible, Tiana followed the two men. Neither man seemed aware that she was nearby.

Once clear of the main room, she set her tray down and was better able to shadow Ashcroft's guest. Within moments, Tiana found herself in another part of the mansion, going down a narrow set of back stairs.

There was nothing to make her think that this part of the thirty-room mansion was any different than the rest of it. But something inside her tensed with each step she took.

For all she knew, she reasoned, the security escort could be taking the guest to an illegal poker game in the extravagantly finished basement. Or maybe to an area where guests could get high in peace.

Although viable, neither scenario worked for her. Her gut told her this was about sex trafficking, maybe because she *needed* to find Janie, and soon, before all trace of her sister was made to disappear, along with all the other girls.

This *had* to be the right place.

She saw the security escort and the guest stop before a closed door at the end of a long, winding hallway. Tiana pressed herself against a wall, trying to become as small as humanly possible.

The security man took out a key and unlocked the door, then looked around the immediate area before finally opening the door and entering with the guest in tow.

Less than a minute later, the security guard was back out in the hallway, without the guest. He carefully locked the door behind him and left.

Tiana waited until Ashcroft's security man was well clear of the area before she made a move. Satisfied that the man was gone, she crossed quickly to the door, then paused to listen.

She heard nothing coming from the other side. But she had a feeling that either the door was soundproof or if there were any girls to be found there, they might be so drugged that they were unconscious, or close to being paralyzed. As for the guest who had disappeared behind the door, she was fairly certain that she could take him. He presented no threat to her.

Here goes nothing, Tiana thought.

The door was locked. She'd expected nothing less, although it would have been nice to catch a break, she thought wearily. However, this was not an insurmountable obstacle. She'd learned how to pick a lock years ago while still a teenager. To punish her whenever she committed some infraction of the rules he laid down for her and her sister, her father would have the locks on the front door changed, leaving her to spend the night out in the cold. One of his friends on the force took pity on her and showed her how to use a set of skeleton keys. To this day, she was never without them.

Today was no exception.

Easing the door open, to her surprise Tiana discovered that the door didn't lead to a room. It led to a hallway, beyond which were a number of doors.

She had no idea which to try first or what she might find behind them.

Playing odds she had calculated in her head, she tried the doorknob to the second room. It gave. The room was empty, but it gave the appearance of having recently been vacated. The bed was in complete disarray. Someone *had* been there, but they were gone now.

The third room was empty, as well, but unlike the previous room, this one didn't appear to have been recently occupied, then quickly vacated.

The bed looked untouched. It was beginning to appear as if the last guest had been taken somewhere farther down the hallway. Tiana was determined to try every room until she found either the guest, or her sister.

The fourth room, the last one on that side of the hallway, *was* occupied. The man she'd seen following the security man wasn't there, but there was a girl lying facedown on the bed.

She was dressed in pink, her strawberry blonde hair covering any visible portion of her face.

Tiana's heart all but stopped as she quickly entered the room and closed the door behind her. The face might have been obscured, but she knew, *knew* this had to be her sister.

"Janie?" she whispered.

The girl on the bed didn't respond. There was no indication that the female she was talking to was even conscious.

Crossing over quickly to the bed, Tiana gingerly touched the girl's shoulder.

She shrank away, her head still buried in the comforter.

Tiana knew fear when she saw it. Janie had shrunk away exactly like that when she was cringing before their father's wrath.

"Janie?" Tiana repeated in an urgent whisper. "Is that you?"

The girl still didn't respond except to attempt to shrink even farther into the bed.

Tiana's heart told her it was Janie, but even if it wasn't, she couldn't just turn away and leave this girl here like this. Tiana gently placed a hand on each of the girl's slender, bare shoulders and raised her up to look at her.

When the girl finally lifted her head, she stared blankly at her, as if she couldn't process who or what she was seeing.

Janie.

"Oh, my God, what have they done to you, Janie?" Tiana cried in a strangled whisper, horrified at what might have happened to her sister, afraid to let her imagination go. Whatever had been done to her didn't matter right now. The only thing that mattered was getting her sister out of here.

"Can you walk, honey? Can you stand up? Please, baby, try. I've got to get you out of here," she told her sister urgently.

The girl continued to stare at her, but finally, there

seemed to be an inkling of recognition entering the blue eyes. A spark of understanding.

"T?" Janie murmured in confusion, as if she couldn't understand what her sister was doing here in her nightmare.

T.

Tiana's heart all but seized up on her. That was what Janie used to call her when they were little girls, because she couldn't say her whole name. Tiana felt tears welling up in her eyes.

Now wasn't the time, Tiana angrily upbraided herself. She'd cry *after* she got her sister out of here and to some safe area, not before. Right now this *definitely* didn't qualify as a safe area.

"It's me," she told Janie urgently. "C'mon, we've got to get you out of this room before someone comes in."

But as she drew her sister up from the bed, struggling to get her to stand up, Janie collapsed at her feet. Tiana tried getting her up again, but with the same results. Janie's legs seemed rubbery and incapable of sustaining any sort of weight.

"I can't," Janie cried in a hoarse, frustrated voice. "I can't. Go," she ordered, finally beginning to get a glimmer of spirit in her voice. "They'll be back any second. You've got to get out of here."

"Not without you, I don't," Tiana informed her fiercely. Taking hold of Janie's arm, she slung it over her shoulder and held on to it tightly with her other hand as she struggled to get her sister upright. "We're getting out of here together."

"Very noble. I take it you're related."

The smooth, suave voice, coming out of the blue like that, managed to slice through her consciousness. Tiana turned to see that Ashcroft was standing in the doorway, blocking her way out.

"Yes, you're sisters, aren't you?" he said, answering his own question. "I can see the resemblance now. Actually," he confessed, "it struck me when you offered me that goblet of wine from your tray. I have a rather well-developed memory, and I saw immediately that you have the same features." His eyes narrowed onto their target as he looked at her lips. "The same tempting mouth. Except that you're too old for most of my clientele. Their tastes apparently have never fully progressed past high school. Personally, I'm not that restrictive," he said, moving in closer.

Tiana's flesh felt as if it wanted to crawl away. This other side to a man who had been dubbed "Mr. Generosity" was cold and decidedly creepy.

Desperate to save Janie and not wanting to allow Ashcroft to think that he was frightening her, she pointed out to him rather icily, "Then Janie's too old for them, too. She's nineteen."

Ashcroft nodded as he spared Janie a quick, admiring look. "I rather suspected as much," he told her as if they were old friends, sharing a confidence, "but you have to admit, your sister looks younger than her chronological age—her boyfriend swore that she was underage, but then, he was enamored with the 'finder's fee' he thought he was getting.

"Poor thing," he commented, regarding Janie now as if she were an inanimate object, "being handled like so much chattel by that worthless boyfriend of hers. She really should have been a better judge of character," he said, shaking his head.

"That doesn't matter at the moment," Tiana bit off. Did Ashcroft think he could just chat her up, diverting her attention from the real issue? Just how simpleminded were the people he dealt with? "It's over. Don't make things worse for yourself by trying to keep us here."

Ashcroft laughed and it occurred to Tiana that she had never heard a harsher, more chilling sound.

"Oh, my dear, you're right about it being over, but I'm afraid that it's you who's over, not me." Ashcroft cocked his head, looking at her sympathetically. "You must be intelligent enough to understand that. I couldn't be that poor a judge of character—could I?" he asked whimsically.

"People know I'm here," she told him in no uncertain terms, even though, to the best of her knowledge, only Brennan knew and he was only one man. A man who most likely was on the other side of the mansion right now. "It's just a matter of time before—"

"Please, don't insult my intelligence," Ashcroft requested with incredibly polite civility. "No one knows you're here. We both know that. If there *was* an official investigation going on, or something that might eventually lead people to my doorstep, I would have known about it long before this moment. I stay abreast of things like that, because leaving them to chance is worse than foolish. I have people everywhere," he informed her smugly. "And you, my dear, are apparently being a tad dramatic. Well, I'm afraid I must tell you that it won't do you any good."

He watched in amusement as she did her best to get to the door with Janie, who half dragged first one leg, then the other. All the while Janie held on tightly to her waist.

"She's drugged," Ashcroft pointed out needlessly. "How far do you think you'll get?"

"As far as she needs to," Brennan said, his presence filling the doorway to the expensively decorated torture chamber.

Things from that point happened almost too quickly for Tiana to process.

Seeing Brennan here, judging by the expression on Ashcroft's face, the philanthropist knew he had come face-to-face with the end of his elaborately fashioned charade. Fearing exposure, the billionaire grabbed Tiana, yanked her to him and quickly converted her into a human shield for himself as her sister, deprived of support, crumbled to the floor.

He aimed a gun right against Tiana's temple.

"Think again," Ashcroft taunted.

Chapter 18

"You don't want to do this," Brennan told Ashcroft, his eyes never leaving the billionaire's as he trained his handgun on the man.

"You're right, I don't," Ashcroft replied, sounding almost amicable. Even so, his grip around Tiana's waist tightened and the weapon he had remained against her temple. "However, the way I see it, I have no choice. Either I give up everything I've worked for all these years and see my reputation dragged through the mud, or I eliminate the two witnesses who have it in their power to destroy everything that I am."

"You took care of that yourself," Tiana snapped at him, her anger getting the better of her.

"Maybe, maybe not," Ashcroft allowed. He glanced at the girl on the floor and must have decided she wasn't a threat. Brennan was much more forbidable at that moment. "But the question right now is how to fix this. Giving up is not an option here," he told Brennan.

"Death by cop isn't exactly a feel-good alternative," Brennan countered. The tension within the room was mounting quickly.

"Oh, but I don't intend to die," Ashcroft said to Brennan. "In case it hasn't hit you, that would require you taking one hell of a shot, Detective. Are you that good?" he asked, his tone mocking him. "Put your weapon down on the floor and maybe I'll let her live."

"Brennan, don't do it," Tiana cried. "Don't put down your weapon! He'll kill all three of us. Shoot him!"

"I wouldn't chance it if I were you," Ashcroft told him, shifting Tiana so that she blocked most of him. All except for the fact that he was about three inches taller than she was.

"But you're not me."

The gun Brennan had kept leveled on Ashcroft went off as he fired one well-aimed bullet directly into the center of Ashcroft's forehead. The second the bullet exploded, Tiana lunged forward, clear of the man even as he sank down on the floor, an utterly surprised expression frozen on his lean, patrician face.

Tiana stared at Brennan, wide-eyed. That was an incredible shot, given his vantage point. "You killed him," Tiana cried.

"Had to. If I'd just wounded him, he would have gotten his shot in and that would have been you lying on the floor right there instead of him." His eyes all but devoured her. She was all right, he assured himself. She was all right. "I picked him. That okay with you?" he asked, sounding almost laid-back about what had just transpired.

She saw no point in acting nonchalant. "That's *wonderful* with me."

His concern got the better of him for a moment. "Are you really all right?" he asked her solicitously.

Tiana allowed herself just ten seconds to exhale and pull herself together. "Yes, thanks to you." And then she was turning toward her sister, trying to drag Janie to her feet. Brennan gently moved her out of the way and picked up the unconscious girl, placing her on the bed.

"I don't know what he gave her, but he really drugged her. She's completely out of it," she told Brennan. "I tried talking to her, but I don't know how much she absorbed."

"The hospital should be able to figure it out," he assured her. "There're more girls in the rooms around the corner down the hall. The place is honeycombed with them. We hit the mother lode. Looks like Ashcroft wanted one last hurrah before he had the girls smuggled out of the country." He took out his cell phone to call in Duncan and what was by now the rest of his backup.

She had to know. Tiana put her hand on his cell phone, interrupting his call. "How did you happen to appear just in the nick of time?"

He looked at her, amused. "Complaining?"

"Oh, God, no, just curious."

He pressed a few numbers on his keypad and listened to a phone ring on the other end. Once it was picked up, all he said was "Come now. It's over." Getting Duncan's confirmation that he was on his way, Brennan put his phone away and told her, "I could say it was magnificent timing."

"You could, but it wouldn't be the truth." Brennan didn't strike her as the type to leave things up to chance like that. "This end of the mansion is just littered with rooms. Just how did you pick the right one at the right time?" she asked.

"I used a tracking device."

"On me?" she asked incredulously. "What kind of tracking device?" And just how had he managed to pin it on her person without her noticing it, or having it set off any alarms?

"The kind that works," he told her drolly.

"Brennan." She stretched his name out, a warning tone in her voice. Her nerves stretched to their full capacity, she wasn't in the mood for word games.

Brennan made up his mind to tell her everything. There was no point not to. "You know when I told you not to do anything too stupid?"

"Yes."

"Well, I did give your arm a squeeze," he reminded her.

"Yes?" She was still waiting for a plausible explanation.

"That was so you wouldn't notice I was planting a tracking device on your person." He could see that she was struggling with accepting this information, with being kept in the dark about something so blatant. "I wasn't about to risk having something happen to you," he said fiercely.

"Oh?" she asked, picking up something in his voice that made her stop and take stock of the situation, of what they had between them.

"The report about a partner's murder has to be done in triplicate," he deadpanned. "I'm a man of action. I'm not a typist. I'd be at the station all night."

She nodded, her tone matching his. "Well, can't have that."

He looked at her for a long moment, allowing himself to lightly touch a strand of hair that fell into her eyes. "Not when I have someplace better to be."

She nodded, telling herself not to melt right here. Not yet. "Which would be anywhere but behind a desk, filling out forms."

"I was thinking of someplace more specific," he said. "Like my place—with you. Now that this is finally over, I can show you where I really live—if you're interested," he added, watching to see her reaction.

"Oh, I am." She glanced over toward her sister. Janie was still unconscious. "But I need to get Janie checked out first."

"That goes without saying," he agreed. A commotion had him reaching for the gun he'd holstered. Tiana was quick to pick up the gun that Ashcroft had dropped. Both weapons were trained at the door when it opened again.

Duncan stopped dead in his tracks, pushing Valri behind him before either of them realized what was actually happening. "Is that any way to treat backup that *you* sent for?"

"Sorry, just a little edgy," Brennan confessed, holstering his weapon again.

"Understandable," Duncan allowed. "You all right?" he asked, looking from his brother to the woman who had accompanied him on this mission.

Before either could answer, Duncan looked down at the dead man on the floor. His mouth dropped open. "Oh, hell, is that…?"

"One and the same," Brennan told him.

"You mean *he's* the one behind all this?" Valri asked, stunned.

"That's the way this played out," Brennan told his sister. He glanced back at the man who had built up as well as destroyed so many lives. It was the perfect cover, he couldn't help thinking. "Guess he was a little too self-made for his own good."

By the sound of the indignant protests, reinforced by echoes of running feet, police personnel were flooding the entire mansion, leaving no room untouched. Festive party attendees turned into shocked and angry detainees until everything could be sorted out.

Ambulances arrived to take the girls who were found chained and held captive to several different hospitals in the immediate vicinity.

Tiana accompanied her sister within the ambulance that was taking Janie to the closest hospital.

"I'll meet you there," Brennan called after her as a paramedic shut the doors. She nodded in response, but the truth of it was she really didn't expect him to follow through on his promise.

She was fairly confident that Brennan would get caught up in filing his report and all the rest of it. Because he'd discharged his gun, he was going to have to surrender the weapon to have it checked out—it was a matter of routine policy.

She doubted if there would be any problem regarding the shooting. On the contrary, this had to be a rather large feather in his cap, as the trite saying went. She was glad for him. He deserved to be recognized for his bravery.

She held Janie's hand the entire trip in. She was still unconscious since she'd collapsed onto the floor in the mansion. Tiana knew it might be a futile endeavor, but she was determined to get through to her sister on some level, and this seemed like the easiest way.

Who knew, maybe gripping her hand like that would somehow cause Janie to maintain and reestablish her hold on life.

At least it was worth a try.

It seemed like absolute *ages* since her sister had looked at her. Tiana was beginning to be really concerned.

Just as she was about to go out and corner a physician, Janie's eyelids fluttered. Planting herself right beside the bed, Tiana waited eagerly for Janie to open her eyes.

When she finally did, Tiana felt as if her heart was filled to bursting. "Welcome back," she said to Janie, her throat suddenly clogged with tears. She forced them back, but it wasn't without effort.

Janie stared at her. It was obvious that she was struggling to clear her head. "T?"

"Ah, good, you still know who I am," Tiana said with a relieved smile.

"What happened?" Janie murmured. She attempted to sit up and faltered. "My head feels as if someone used it for bowling."

"Pretty nearly," Tiana said sympathetically. "They made you swallow some pretty potent designer drugs, the kind that knock you out. The doctor ordered an IV drip with something to counteract the effects. That's what's attached to you now," she said, indicating the IV next to the bed. "Don't ask me to repeat the name of the serum. It has more letters than the alphabet. But the doctor promised that you should be back to normal in about a day."

Tears had filled Janie's eyes as she looked at Tiana. "You found me."

Tiana smiled, stroking Janie's hair away from her forehead. "Yes, I found you. Hey, was there ever any doubt that I would? You're my baby sister. Nobody gets to order you around but me."

Tears were rolling down the side of her face. "But I told you—"

Taking a tissue from a dispenser near the bed, Tiana wiped away the tracks of her sister's tears. "To go to a very warm place, yes, I know," she said, recalling their last conversation before Janie had disappeared.

"Didn't like it there. Decided to go to wherever you were going instead."

"Wayne…?" Janie asked hoarsely.

"Won't be bothering you anymore," Tiana promised stoically. "Someone decided they didn't want to pay him in cash."

Janie took a breath before trying to frame the question. "Is he—?"

Tiana nodded. "Yes, he is," she said, anticipating the question and wanting to spare Janie from having to ask it. "Whenever you're ready, we'll go back home." She talked faster, trying to keep Janie's mind from dwelling on Wayne's demise. "I'm sure the university will make allowances for what happened and let you come back into the program—"

Janie cut her off. "I don't want to go back to school, at least, not that school. Too much has happened. Every corner of that campus will remind me what a jerk I was. Please, T, don't make me go back."

Tiana read between the lines and understood. "You want a fresh start?" she asked,

Janie seemed incredibly relieved. "Oh, God, yes."

Tiana paused for a moment, thinking. "Well, we could move down here," she said, casting about for alternatives. "I hear they have a lot of good colleges in this part of California."

Janie looked at her, stunned. "You'd move here for me?"

Tiana didn't want it to sound as if she was making some huge sacrifice and not getting anything out of it herself. The truth of it was, she felt that it was time for a change for both of them.

"For you, and maybe I need a change, too," Tiana told her sister.

"Hey," Janie began, in a voice that was beginning to sound progressively more sleepy, "I want to…"

Anticipating Janie's unfinished thoughts, Tiana replied, "You're welcome," with a smile.

She wasn't sure her sister even heard her. Janie was sound asleep again. Most likely, she would be winking in and out like that for the next twelve hours or so.

Tiana looked toward the chair she'd vacated a few minutes ago and considered hanging around, doing another round of sentry duty, until her sister woke up again. She had a statement to give, but other than that—

She sensed he was there before he ever said a single word.

Turning, she saw Brennan standing in the doorway. Though he hadn't taken a step toward her yet, he seemed to fill up the entire room with his presence. It made her feel safe for possibly the first time in her life. She liked that.

"How long have you been standing there?" she asked, suddenly feeling a surge of emotions spiking through her.

Tiana struggled hard not to just throw her arms around his neck and show how happy she was to see him. Though they were alone for all intents and purposes, this was still a public area and a show of emotion might embarrass him, so she refrained.

"A few minutes," he answered. "How long have you two been talking in code?" he asked, amused.

She waved her hand, dismissing his label. "It's not code. I just happen to know what she's thinking, and given her present condition, I wanted to save her the trouble of having to say anything extra."

He nodded, taking in her explanation as a matter of routine. There was a more important topic he wanted to get to and clarify for his own sake. "You really going to stay down here?" he asked as he made his way into the single-care unit.

That was when she noticed that he was carrying two large containers of coffee. She thought that rather odd for a man who wasn't a die-hard coffee drinker.

Crossing to her, he handed her the covered container of coffee he'd picked up for her on his way over to the hospital.

"After what Janie's been through, I think a change of scenery might not be a bad idea." Taking the lid off the container, she took an extralong, gratifying sip of her coffee, allowing it to wind its way all through her before she continued. "Besides, I really do like the weather down here."

He set his container down on the counter beside the sink. "That the only thing you like down here?"

"I like your uncle," she answered. "Think he might be able to get me a job down here?"

"Don't see why not." He assumed she was referring to the chief of Ds. "He told me the police department could always use someone who's sharp." Until just this minute, he hadn't allowed himself to think past the assignment. But the assignment was over. All that remained were the reports to write.

He was staring at her. Why? Was that a good sign, or a bad one? "What?" she forced herself to ask.

He tested the words out on his tongue, as if that would give the concept shape and make it a reality. "You're staying, huh?"

"Yes. I thought we already established that."

"Any particular reason why you're staying?" he asked, then added the part they were both certain of. "Other than giving your sister a change of venue?"

She felt her way around the subject very slowly, not wanting to take too much for granted just in case that was setting herself up for a fall. "Well, I like the idea that the trees stay mostly green all year-round. I've never been a fan of watching leaves fall."

His eyes remained on hers. "Oh, we've got deciduous trees here, too. Is weather and a different school for your sister the only reason you're going to be relocating?" he pressed.

Was he trying to get her to admit to something—or was he hoping her reasons were as vague as she said so he wouldn't be put on the spot? She didn't know how to read him. "Should there be more?"

The shrug was casual, nonchalant. "Only if you think so."

She wished he was easier to second guess. Mentally flipping a coin, she went with "tails." "Look, if you're worried that I might crowd you—"

The corners of his mouth curved just a little. "*Crowd* isn't exactly the word I had in mind."

"What *was* the word you had in mind, then?" *C'mon, Brennan, give me something to work with here. How much do you really want me to admit?*

He carefully placed his container down again and pulled her into his arms. "I'm going to have to think on that for a while," he said, his expression so solemn that for a moment she thought he was actually being serious.

Okay, let's try a safer subject. "I didn't get a chance to thank you for saving my life. Was that a lucky shot?" she asked. Her gut told her that it wasn't, but she wanted to hear it from him.

"Maybe from your point of view," Brennan allowed.

There was that hint of a smile again. "But not from yours?"

"It's the kind of shot I'm used to making." He wouldn't tell her that for one moment, fear had entered his heart, fear that he wasn't as good as he thought he was. As he had once been.

"Let me guess, you're a sniper."

That had been his title once, before he'd gotten into undercover work for the DEA. "Not currently."

She was determined to nail one detail down about this man. "But you were?"

"Might have been." He smiled into her eyes. Some things were still classified. "Modesty doesn't permit me to talk about it."

The hell with modesty. She needed to know. "SWAT or navy SEAL?"

"Yeah," was all he said.

She sighed. She had a feeling she was playing a losing game. "You always this secretive?"

"Guess that'll be something you'll have to find out on your own." He was lightly massaging her shoulders as he spoke. "By the way, do you really want to show your gratitude to me for saving your life?"

"Yes," she answered, never taking her eyes off his. Her knees were growing progressively weaker.

"Good, because I have just the way for you to show me just how grateful you are."

There went her heart, she thought, into double time. "When do we start?"

The smile took over his entire face. "The second I get you home. My real home," he specified, "not that hotel room."

She nodded. "Sounds good to me."

"Would you two take it outside?" Janie mumbled, surprising them both. "I need my sleep."

Tiana quickly drew closer to her sister. "You were awake the whole time?"

"I think she's back asleep," Brennan said, looking closely at her sister. "Most likely, she's going to stay that way now until tomorrow."

He was telling her it was all right to leave Janie for a few hours. The man really did understand how her mind worked. "Where did you say you parked your vehicle?"

"I didn't." Grinning, he took her hand and said, "Follow me."

"To the ends of the earth," she told him with a laugh.

"Oh, hell, I can't wait." Turning on his heel, he

caught her up in his arms and kissed her, long and hard—like a man who had just found his reason for living.

As she melted against him, Tiana knew in her heart that this was a preview of things to come.

Life, she decided, was very, very good.

Finally.

Epilogue

The noise level within the large rambling house and even larger backyard continued to rise. Nobody really seemed to notice. This was a festive occasion and festive occasions came with noise.

Andrew Cavanaugh, completely recovered and ready to demonstrate that happy fact by getting back into the full swing of things, was tackling one of his very favorite excuses for a party: a wedding reception.

At first glance, to the virgin attendee, it looked as if the immediate world had been invited and had decided to RSVP "Yes."

It was only after a little more close scrutiny was applied that it became apparent that the people attending were mostly family or friends—usually both.

Finding a place to park had been a very real challenge. Tiana and Brennan had had to walk back several blocks in order to get to the center of the activities.

"Maybe I shouldn't have let you talk me into this," Tiana said uncertainly as they entered the house. She felt like an interloper. From the looks of it, everyone seemed to know everyone else.

Taking her arm to escort her in—and to keep her from bolting in case that crossed her mind—Brennan laughed. "As if anyone could ever talk you into anything. You wanted to come," he pointed out knowingly.

She had because she'd never had a family, other than Janie, and the idea of a close one, albeit a very large one, intrigued her. But she'd had no idea that there were *this* many of them.

"I feel as if I'm invading," she confessed. "I don't even know the bride or groom."

"No, you don't," he agreed. "But you know me, you know Duncan and Valri—and Uncle Sean. Your boss, the head of the day-shift crime lab," he prompted when she gave no sign of recognizing his last reference.

Embarrassed and somewhat overwhelmed as she wove her way to the backyard with Brennan gently guiding her, she nodded.

"Right." She looked at him a little uneasily. She was *not* going to remember half these names. "Do they come with name badges?"

"No, but you have me and I have a pretty good memory. In my former line of work, it was essential," he reminded her. "I'll let you in on a secret," he said, whispering into her ear as they walked out into the backyard. Evidently, they had arrived at the reception just a beat after the newest happy couple had made their way in. "This is my first Cavanaugh wedding."

And he sincerely hoped, slanting a glance toward her, that it wasn't going to be his last.

"She really is a beautiful bride," Tiana commented with sincerity as she looked at Ashley now, standing next to a beaming Shane Cavanaugh. The latter was holding a baby in his arms as naturally as if she were a part of him. They made a beautiful couple, she thought. "Is that baby theirs?"

Brennan glanced in the direction that she was looking in. "In every way possible but blood."

Her brow furrowed as she turned her head back to look at Brennan. "You're going to have to explain that."

She wasn't familiar with their background, he realized. He'd just taken the fact that she was for granted. "It's a long story, but the short version is that the baby's mother was killed and the infant was kidnapped. Shane and Ashley worked the case together. They finally tracked down the kidnapper, but once the baby was recovered, they found that the infant had no family. There was literally no one to take her in.

"Ashley had grown up an orphan herself—her parents were both killed in an auto accident when she was a toddler—and she couldn't bear to have the baby they'd saved go through what she had, so she petitioned to adopt her."

Brennan paused, glancing back at the happy couple, both of whom, in his opinion, looked absolutely radiant. Knowing what they had both been through, he still envied them their happiness.

"What's the baby's name?" Tiana asked.

"Ashley named her Joy because she said it felt like heaven to hold the baby in her arms."

Tiana smiled. "Sounds like a really nice story."

"Yeah," he agreed. "Complete with a 'happily ever after' to it."

"You believe in that." It was more of a stunned comment than an out-and-out question on her part. She waited for his response, really curious to hear what he had to say.

"Hey, how can't I?" he asked. "All the Cavanaughs have a hundred percent batting average when it comes to marriages."

Something else she hadn't been aware of. She looked around again. This time, things like a passing caress, a quick kiss or affectionate laughter, caught her attention. "Really?"

"Really," he confirmed.

Tiana sighed. "Must be nice." She wasn't even aware of saying the words out loud until she heard them.

"Must be," he agreed. Then, gathering his courage to him—why going ahead to broach what he was about to ask seemed to require more nerve than risking his life by going undercover he had no idea, but he could feel his nerves all standing at attention—he asked her, "Would you like to find out firsthand?"

Tiana wasn't sure where he was going with this and she wasn't going to allow herself to speculate because she didn't like coming face-to-face with disappointment if she could possibly help it. She'd had enough to last a lifetime. *Two* lifetimes.

"You mean by talking to one of the couples?" she asked him.

He watched her carefully. She understood perfectly well what he meant, he thought, but he could understand her being cautious. "No, by becoming one of the couples."

Her eyes widened. "Wait, slow down," she cried.

"If I slowed down any more, I'd be going backward," Brennan patiently pointed out.

"Are you asking me to marry you?" she asked in a hushed, disbelieving whisper.

"Yes. By the way," he prompted, "that is the operative word here. *Yes* in case you missed it." He knew he had to give her a way out, so he added, "Unless you don't want to, in which case don't say anything, just change the subject and let me nurse my wounds quietly in some corner."

Tiana stood staring at him, stunned. The world had come to a complete halt about thirty seconds ago, right up to making the vast crowd around them completely disappear into some nether, invisible world.

Half convinced she'd imagined all this, Tiana took a deep breath.

But Brennan was still there.

And so was she.

"You know," she began slowly, "for a very smart man, you can be awful stupid."

"Wait, is this going to end well or badly?" he asked. "I need to be prepared."

"You need to have your head examined," she contradicted with a laugh. She felt like Cinderella being swept away by the prince. "But while we're waiting for that, yes, I'll marry you." The moment she said it, she had this overwhelming urge to repeat it—so she did. "Yes, I will marry you," she cried, this time more loudly.

She would have said it a third time, louder still, but was prevented by the fact that her lips were now completely covered by his.

And she couldn't have been happier about it.

* * * * *

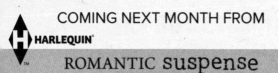

COMING NEXT MONTH FROM

HARLEQUIN®

ROMANTIC suspense

Available June 3, 2014

#1803 OPERATION UNLEASHED
Cutter's Code • by Justine Davis

Drew offers to marry his brother's widow and care for her son, though he never expects to fall for Alyssa. But when the child is kidnapped, Drew will do whatever it takes to make his family whole again.

#1804 SPECIAL OPS RENDEZVOUS
The Adair Legacy • by Karen Anders

After surviving torture, soldier Sam Winston sees threats everywhere. When his politician mother is almost killed, he teams up with his psychiatrist, the mysterious Olivia, to find the assassin. Except Olivia is keeping a secret....

#1805 PROTECTING HER ROYAL BABY
The Mansfield Brothers • by Beth Cornelison

As Brianna Coleman suffers amnesia, Hunter Mansfield vows to protect her...even when her baby proves to be royalty hunted by international assassins. But can he protect his heart?

#1806 LONE STAR REDEMPTION
by Colleen Thompson

When Jessie Layton arrives seeking her missing twin, rancher Zach Rayford defends his mother's lies. Together, they confront dangerous secrets, including the parentage of the "miracle child" holding Zach's family together.

HRSCNM0514

REQUEST YOUR FREE BOOKS!
2 FREE NOVELS PLUS 2 FREE GIFTS!

ROMANTIC suspense

Sparked by danger, fueled by passion

YES! Please send me 2 FREE Harlequin® Romantic Suspense novels and my 2 FREE gifts (gifts are worth about $10). After receiving them, if I don't wish to receive any more books, I can return the shipping statement marked "cancel." If I don't cancel, I will receive 4 brand-new novels every month and be billed just $4.74 per book in the U.S. or $5.24 per book in Canada. That's a savings of at least 14% off the cover price! It's quite a bargain! Shipping and handling is just 50¢ per book in the U.S. and 75¢ per book in Canada.* I understand that accepting the 2 free books and gifts places me under no obligation to buy anything. I can always return a shipment and cancel at any time. Even if I never buy another book, the two free books and gifts are mine to keep forever.

240/340 HDN F45N

Name _____ (PLEASE PRINT)

Address _____ Apt. #

City _____ State/Prov. _____ Zip/Postal Code

Signature (if under 18, a parent or guardian must sign)

Mail to the **Harlequin® Reader Service:**
IN U.S.A.: P.O. Box 1867, Buffalo, NY 14240-1867
IN CANADA: P.O. Box 609, Fort Erie, Ontario L2A 5X3

Want to try two free books from another line?
Call 1-800-873-8635 or visit www.ReaderService.com.

* Terms and prices subject to change without notice. Prices do not include applicable taxes. Sales tax applicable in N.Y. Canadian residents will be charged applicable taxes. Offer not valid in Quebec. This offer is limited to one order per household. Not valid for current subscribers to Harlequin Romantic Suspense books. All orders subject to credit approval. Credit or debit balances in a customer's account(s) may be offset by any other outstanding balance owed by or to the customer. Please allow 4 to 6 weeks for delivery. Offer available while quantities last.

Your Privacy—The Harlequin® Reader Service is committed to protecting your privacy. Our Privacy Policy is available online at www.ReaderService.com or upon request from the Harlequin Reader Service.

We make a portion of our mailing list available to reputable third parties that offer products we believe may interest you. If you prefer that we not exchange your name with third parties, or if you wish to clarify or modify your communication preferences, please visit us at www.ReaderService.com/consumerschoice or write to us at Harlequin Reader Service Preference Service, P.O. Box 9062, Buffalo, NY 14269. Include your complete name and address.

HRS13R

SPECIAL EXCERPT FROM

H HARLEQUIN®

ROMANTIC suspense

When Drew offers to marry his brother's widow and care for her son, he never expects to fall for Alyssa. But when the child is kidnapped, Drew will do whatever it takes to make his family whole again.

Read on for a sneak peek at

OPERATION UNLEASHED

by Justine Davis, available June 2014 from Harlequin® Romantic Suspense.

"We did this."

Her voice was soft, almost a whisper from behind him. He spun around. She'd gone up with Luke to get him warm and dry, and set him up with his current favorite book. He was already reading well for his age, on to third-grade level readers, and Drew knew that was thanks to Alyssa. "Yes," he said, his voice nearly as quiet as hers. "We did."

"It has to stop, Drew."

"Yes."

"What can I do to make that easier?"

God, he hated this. She was being so reasonable, so understanding. And he felt like a fool because the only answer he had was "Stop loving my brother."

"I'm not Luke," he said, not quite snapping. "Don't treat me like a six-year-old."

"Luke," she said sweetly, "is leaving temper tantrums behind."

He drew back sharply. Opened his mouth, ready to truly snap this time. And stopped.

"Okay," he said after a moment, "I had that one coming."

"Yes."

In an odd way, her dig pleased him. Not because it was accurate, he sheepishly admitted, but because she felt confident enough to do it. She'd been so weak, sick and scared when he'd found her four years ago, going toe-to-toe with him like this would have been impossible. But she was strong now, poised and self-assured. And he took a tiny bit of credit for that.

"You've come a long way," he said quietly.

"Because I don't cower anymore?"

He frowned. "I never made you cower."

For an instant she looked startled. "I never said you did. You saved us, Drew, don't think I don't know that, or will ever forget it. I have come a long way, and it's in large part because you made it possible."

It was a pretty little speech, a sentiment she'd expressed more than once. And not so long ago it had been enough. More than enough. It had told him he'd done exactly what he'd intended. That he'd accomplished his goal. That she was stable now, strong, and he'd had a hand in that.

And it wasn't her fault that wasn't enough for him anymore.

**Don't miss
OPERATION UNLEASHED
by Justine Davis,
available June 2014 from
Harlequin® Romantic Suspense.**

ROMANTIC suspense

SPECIAL OPS RENDEZVOUS
by Karen Anders

The Adair Legacy

Heartstopping danger, breathtaking passion, conspiracy and intrigue. **The Adair Legacy** has it all.

After surviving torture, soldier Sam Winston sees threats everywhere. But when his politician mother is almost killed, he teams up with his psychiatrist, the mysterious Olivia, to find the assassin. Except Olivia is keeping a secret....

Look for *SPECIAL OPS RENDEZVOUS* by Karen Anders in June 2014. Available wherever books and ebooks are sold.

Don't miss other titles from **The Adair Legacy** miniseries:
HIS SECRET, HER DUTY by Carla Cassidy
EXECUTIVE PROTECTION by Jennifer Morey

Heart-racing romance, high-stakes suspense!

www.Harlequin.com

ROMANTIC suspense

PROTECTING HER ROYAL BABY
by Beth Cornelison

The Mansfield Brothers

A woman in labor. A man on a mission.
The Mansfield Brothers series continues...

As Brianna Coleman suffers amnesia, Hunter
Mansfield vows to protect her...even when her baby
proves to be royalty hunted by international assassins.
He'll do anything, pay the ultimate price if necessary,
for one chance to save the woman he loves and her
royal baby. But can he protect his heart?

Look for *PROTECTING HER ROYAL BABY* from
The Mansfield Brothers series by Beth Cornelison
in June 2014. Available wherever books and
ebooks are sold.

Also from *The Mansfield Brothers* miniseries by
Beth Cornelison: *THE RETURN OF CONOR MANSFIELD*

Available wherever ebooks are sold.

Heart-racing romance, high-stakes suspense!

www.Harlequin.com

HRS27875

HARLEQUIN®

ROMANTIC suspense
LONE STAR REDEMPTION
by Colleen Thompson

Rusted Spur, Texas...
where passion meets suspense!

Desperate to reunite her missing twin with her dying
mother, Jessie Layton arrives at the Rayford ranch with
all the questions a good journalist would ask—plus
three more: Why is Zach, the extremely handsome
son, defending his mother's obvious lies?
Who is the "miracle child" they dote on?
And why is Zach so hostile?

But even as they spar, the reporter and the rancher
fight a growing attraction, intensified by the lethal
danger following Jessie. Together they risk their lives
confronting secrets that could destroy Zach's family...
if he chooses to tell the truth and do right by the
headstrong woman who's corralled him!

Look for *LONE STAR REDEMPTION*
by Colleen Thompson in June 2014.
Available wherever books and ebooks are sold.

Heart-racing romance, high-stakes suspense!

www.Harlequin.com

HRS27876

Love the Harlequin book you just read?

Your opinion matters.

Review this book on your favorite book site, review site, blog or your own social media properties and share your opinion with other readers!

Be sure to connect with us at:
Harlequin.com/Newsletters
Facebook.com/HarlequinBooks
Twitter.com/HarlequinBooks